THE PARIS MATCH

the Paris Match

Collected Stories

Pandora Dylan Gorman

Published by The Rose Press

Designed by Vince Pannullo
Printed in the United States of America
by RJ Communications.

ISBN: 978-0-578-20347-8

Contents

This book is dedicated to

Mab Ashforth, an extraordinary

woman who really knew how to love.

More

"I feel more porteño than Argentine."

Jorge Luis Borges.

Philippa was never happy with her name and it came in useful when she wanted to dress like a boy. The short dark hair looked good on her and she looked well in the navy blue St. Laurent suit she had fitted in Paris and the white tuxedo shirt with long cuffs. She enjoyed looking androgynous and when she was out in the bars at night she never had to think up a name for herself.

- Hi, I'm Phil, she would say and shake your hand like an American.

*

The sun was hot. The Roman heat was intolerable. Charles sat at an outside table. He was sweating in a white suit while drinking gin and tonic. There were other people at the café. It was three o'clock in the afternoon and no one was moving to get back to work in the heat of the day. They would open their shops again at six and their offices at seven. Valerie sat across from him drinking mint tea stirring a lot of sugar into it and licking the spoon. She wore her usual black outfit and a straw hat with a wide brim.

- I've always wanted to go to Harry's Bar, she said.
- One of these evenings, we'll go over there, Charles said.
- Wouldn't Philippa like to go?
- No, I don't think so. That's not her kind of place.
- What's her kind of place? Valerie asked.
- I wouldn't know, Charles said.

Charles wiped his forehead with the white napkin and searched for the waiter. He was impatient to go although he wouldn't see his sister today. Philippa was off hanging about some theatre somewhere with some people and had promised to phone. He wanted to get back to the hotel. He really hated Rome. It reminded him of Latin America when he had lived there with his father for a time when they were getting the ranch going.

His father was a man of business acumen who forecasted oil and water rights. He moved about the world negotiating the buying of properties. He saw potential where no one else did at the time and was willing to take risks. He had some disasters but mostly he was not wrong. This wandering ambition made for an interesting life for him and his family.

Staying in North America and growing up like his friends would have been fine with Charles. He was often in boarding school or off with his father in some undesired place wanting to be at home with his mother in New York until she moved with her Argentine husband to Buenos Aires once her Haitian divorce was final. She had married an unpleasant man and that wasn't so attractive. Mostly Charles avoided her. The things he hated about Latin America were innumerable and the first and most painful was that he was not at home!

Gone were the tall gray buildings of New York City and the cool green lawns of The Hamptons, also the dark blue grass of Bermuda where he had spent his summers lolling about in white tennis clothes on the lawns along with his friends. Gone was the big pink house on the harbor that had served as Eugene O' Neil's home before it came into his father's hands. This fact interested his sister Philippa alone and she often sat in the study reading or writing in her notebooks looking out at the sea and the sky imagining the playwright. She would be famous too. She suffered because she was a writer, she decided. She wrote a bad novel. Her father laughed at it. She sat in the study that led off of her father's room with two steps you had to watch out for when it was dark Encased here as in Proust's cork room it was said O' Neil had written *Morning Becomes Electra* in the cedar lined study looking out over the harbor and the gray Atlantic Ocean.

*

In the north of Argentina Charles stayed in the austere stonewashed sienna ranch house surrounded by thick trees. The place was populated with mosquitos as large as small birds and raindrops the size of teacups when it poured. He slept under the mosquito nets dreaming of parties in New York on the rooftops of his friends' penthouses and woke up in the mornings to the smell of the cardamom Arabic coffee from the kitchen. At night there were bats squeaking and flying about if you lay awake trying to sleep while the scent of jasmine and lily wafted in with the wind. During the day he tried to imitate his father and walked about in breeches and long boots although he never went near a horse.

Charles preferred the ranch in the south. The huge house was whitewashed with lime and had the usual red tile roof and ceramic floors to keep it cool where there are no trees. The estancia's main house sat in the middle of orange, lemon, lime, and olive groves. The kitchen garden contained tomatoes, potatoes, and peas which were brought to the table each night on platters piled high when they had their *bifes* or steaks at dinner. It had taken decades to grow these gardens! The pampas region outside of Buenos Aires is pale flat empty land as far as the eye can see unlike the northern provinces with their jungle and marsh good for growing the country's rice and tea Here his friends visited for *asados* or barbecues often. They flew in from the neighboring ranches in small planes landing on the crude airstrip. The ranch hands we would call cowboys also called gauchos rode alongside the plane to guide it in after landing. They waived their hats at the pilot to guide them in and cantered ahead.

Philippa had been away at school often which is where Charles believed the trouble began. He was prone to saying, otherwise she would never be like this. No one had ever reported her for anything at school and Philippa when she was younger had been quite the academic phenom in the family, in the school and in the region. She was the youngest student and the first female ever to have achieved the highest examination results for overseas students from the British examination board before she reached the age of fourteen. By the time she was fifteen she had been on her way to university in England. It was during her first year that she stopped returning Charles' calls when he was in London.

One day he ran into her in the street. She was coming out of a pub in Kensington with a man and she was laughing hysterically. He saw that she was slightly embarrassed as she would not look him straight in the face. He had stood in front of her.

- What are you doing down here? Why aren't you up at school? he asked her.

  He looked at her wearing odd clothes in his opinion; she had on a man's suit, fingerless gloves, high heeled gold cowboy boots and a fake fur shrug. The worst thing he saw was her hair which was a jumble of black and red striped dreadlocks teased into an impossible high mess and stuck with little silver clips shaped like birds or music notes.
- Philippa what are you doing here? And why don't you return my calls?

  She laughed.
- This is my brother Charles. School is so boring. I had to get away.
- She needed to get away to London, her companion said.

- It's so dull, she said. Philippa had a British accent now.
- Who are you? Charles said.
- Charles, this is Christophe., she said, Christophe this is Charles. .
- Pleased to meet you, Charles said without really opening his mouth at all.
  They didn't shake hands.
- When are you going back? Don't you have exams in two weeks? he asked her
- I'm on my way back up this afternoon and yes, I have exams, she said.
- Is this how you always dress now? he said.
- Oh, please. She gave him a kiss on the cheek and waved her hand in annoyance.
- We're going now. I have to go to another place.
  She walked away and Charles shouted realizing she did not smell of alcohol at all.
- I'm coming up this weekend then, he shouted.
- Yes, yes! She yelled back. She laughed again as if she couldn't stop as if nothing could ever be so funny again still holding on to the man's arm. She had always been a quiet, serious girl and this laughter made her seem the giddy opposite.

*

- Oxford is really quite the place, Valerie said to Philippa, your whole future will be made, if you just stick it out there.

- What do you mean? Philippa asked.
- Well, I mean you can have any job you want. You'll have the world at your feet once you graduate, she told her watching the crowd saunter by .She was drinking the usual mint tea.
- Nonsense, said Philippa.

Philippa was silent for a few minutes. She pretended to watch the people joining the crowd already seated at the café. The café was bursting with energy and the air about the tables hummed with conversation. Valerie felt uncomfortable in the silence at her table.

- Everything I want in life is denied me, said Philippa slowly. I did not leave because I wanted to. I left because I can't work legally in England and my parents have cut off my money. My father says suddenly that my education is pretentious. A woman doesn't need to go to college. My mother has decided she doesn't want me to continue as her husband thinks that's best.
- Have you told the school? Valerie asked. I mean, they just can't do this to you!
- I can't tell them I have no more money. Instead I said I'd changed my mind and that life is university. That I had decided to leave. Needless to say it was considered disgraceful.

Valerie had nothing. She watched her sister-in-law stir her

lemon soda with a long spoon as she stared out at the piazza. Philippa studied the blur that was the Bernini fountain in the middle of the piazza or plaza as they say in Argentina. It's water flowed from the Acqua Virgo acqueduct just like the other two fountains in the square.It was early evening in Piazza Navona and people were crossing in front of them. The café was full outside. The evening sky was heartbreaking and even near-sighted Philippa could see the watercolor streaks of blues and yellows in the sky above the buildings and the Four Seasons fountain in the square. Her eyes filled with tears as she felt the longing for Buenos Aires again.

Philippa was too slim now, gaunt in the face so that she resembled the woman in Picasso's Repas Frugal. Her face was drawn and it made her look older than she was. She had cut her hair very short so that her cheekbones stood out and her nose was more pronounced. She had very large eyes and when she looked at you she did not really see you as she was very myopic. This made her able to appear to give great eye contact. She was always pleasant to talk to as she seemed so interested. In fact she was no less fascinated than she appeared. It was her vision she could not focus. She was able to focus her attention.

*

She stayed in Rome in a small apartment on the Via del Moro. It was in the quarter known as Trastevere and was a few minutes walk from the Tiber. She could cross the Ponte Sisto and be in Piazza Navona in twenty minutes on foot. At the apartment people were constantly dropping by and sometimes she needed to get away from the constant flow of visitors. She had her favorites among them Joe Worth from Texas, Marcelo from the outskirts of Rome, Angelo the theology student, Giulio Marzio the actor, and David in the Army. Some men would telephone her and sometimes they just stopped by and rang the bell downstairs from the street. She would throw down the key to the heavy front door wrapped inside a leather glove onto the cobblestones and they would let themselves in and climb the narrow white marble stairs to the third floor. She would make tea and they would bring her cakes, pastries, whiskey, vodka, tequila, rare gin, beer, cigarettes, chocolates, English language magazines, coffee, bottles of Coca Cola which she liked and drank with wedges of lemon and ice. Of course bottles of wine and travel souvenirs from everywhere, clothes, books, some jewelry and always they gave her money. She had some friends who were businessmen though they usually asked her to visit them in their hotels and for them she would take taxis.

When she was not writing in her journals in black fountain pen her daily impressions of Rome and her recordings of her internal dialogue she was reading. For this reason she often liked to be alone. There was nothing better in the world than getting up to the early cries of *Aoh* in the Via del Moro and to the sun lighting up the gold and orange buildings through half closed shutters, making tea and sitting all morning with a book. She read all the things she had no time to read in school. She read whatever she wanted with no reason for it.

She read in English, Spanish, in Portuguese, Italian, and French. She regretted she could not read in Russian to read Tolstoy, Dostoevsky and Turgenev in their original language. She read the novels of Balzac in English, French and German. She spent much as she had in England every bit of income on paperbacks and cigarettes and the bus only now the source of funds was no longer a check for fifty pounds in allowance from her mother sent from Argentina each month.

Her bedroom was lined with shelves along which stood for example the works of George Eliot, Honoré de Balzac, Paul Bowles, Virginia Woolf , Charlotte Bronte, Emily Bronte, Thomas Hardy, Thomas Mann, Charles Dickens, Henry Fielding, Somerset Maugham, Evelyn Waugh, Julio Cortazar, Ernesto Sabato, Luisa Valenzuela, Cicero, Seneca, Milton, Shakespeare, Marlowe, Arthur Miller, Pier Paolo Passolini, Sophocles, Jorge Amado, Alan Patton and John -David Morley. Luisa Valenzuela just about every volume she could get her hands on of this author and some very expensive hardback imported editions.

*

Charles made his way back to the Prince of Wales hotel and asked at the desk and found there were no messages. He went upstairs to take a nap in the cool dark room without Valerie. She was out still window shopping and walking in the city. He lay down on the antique wooden bed on top of the linen sheets in his clothes.

His father had married a very wealthy woman at a time

when he had experienced a decline in his financial good fortune. Lawrence and Olympia Silverman owned a house together in the best section of Houston, Texas, a ranch in the south of the state, a working cattle ranch in Colorado, a house in New York, and an apartment in London. His father had sold the famous house in Bermuda, and bought the ranch in Eagle, Colorado thirty minutes outside of Vail with its own airstrip for Eagle Airport. It was a beautiful place and easy to get to and they invited their friends from Houston and New York often. The main ranch house was always full of people and the gatherings there were talked of among the local people. The ranch employed a manager and many working cowboys to handle the cattle and all the ranch work.

Charles' stepmother Olympia was intelligent and socially ambitious. It was her idea that Charles should go to Europe to bring back Philippa. She thought his sister's life as a lost ex patriot had gone too far. Charles and his wife left for Europe with all their travel expenses paid for by Lawrence Silverman. Olympia had convinced his father this is what he should do and Lawrence did it to look good to her. He was in no hurry to have his daughter back home although it was a constant annoyance to him that she was not under his control. He had told her getting her degree at Oxford was pretentious. He had indicated that women should not go to college anyhow as it was unnecessary for them. He was reluctant to pay for her education at any point in her life and left that to her mother even when he was a millionaire several times over. He thought that should be financed through the trust fund left by her maternal grandmother. Her mother was soon convinced by her new husband to cut off Philippa's money and she was forced to withdraw from university.

*

Finally, she called.

- Meet us for drinks, she said.
- Who' s us?
- Me and Lorena. You'll like her. Trust me.
- Trust you? He sneered. Why should I trust you?
- Come on, be nice. It looks like we're going to the Montreux Jazz festival!
- I can't wait, he said.
- Really? She said.
- Well anything's gotta be better than Rome. Switzerland is at least healthier than Italy. The Swiss are rich industrious people. Maybe I can talk some sense into you there. It's just like Buenos Aires here. Everyone's lazy here, just drifting along.
- Do you really hate it so much here?
- I'm not going to answer that, Charles said, I've made myself clear. Now how about those drinks?

*

It was mid-winter when she arrived at Oxford by train with her suitcase and her guitar. A rare snowfall covered the domes and spires in places. Patches of gold and needles of silver glittered in the pale morning sky. The future called to her attentively through light scattered clouds from the depths of infinity. At the sight of the old stone buildings at the domes and spires of the churches and colleges rising up against a gray and white sky she felt an intense melancholy.

She had worked towards this day for many years. Intense beauty would always have the effect of making her feel deep sadness.

She found the college where she would stay for her university entrance exams and there was some confusion about the room. The house mother had to find out what had happened and when she showed her the door to her room it was clear her name had been scratched out.

- Oh! I think we thought you weren't coming! The woman said to appease her and to indicate the correct attitude towards this slight.
  The girls inside barely greeted her until the house mother took charge saying in a loud voice barely warranted in the small room for four
- This is Philippa. She is here after all. I expect you to help her get settled in here.
- Thank you, said Philippa staring at the three girls who were staring back at her.
- Hello, I'm Elise, said one girl smiling politely at her, do come in.
- I'm Annette, said another girl, your bed is over there, she pointed out to her.
- I'm Minnie, said a friendly voice and this girl's face

was open and radiant like a child or the young Dalai Lama.

- Pleased to meet you, she said to each of them.
- But you sound English, Elise said.
- I've been to British schools in Argentina, Philippa answered her.

When it was established that she was an American the whole mood changed.

- Oh my God, you're American! screamed Minnie. Oh my God! Oh my God!
- So you are, said Elise.
- How thrilling, said Annette generously.
- Darling, Elise said to Philippa, we thought you were a wog.
- What's that? Philippa asked.
- Someone we wouldn't want in our room, Elise said.
- Someone from South America, Minnie added gaily.
- Someone who is black, said Elise.
- That's all rot, Annette said turning away.
- Annette's taste in men is well, rather exotic if you must know, Elise said.
- Fuck off, Elise.
- Sorry, darling.
- Are you doing music? Minnie asked her.
- No, unless I can't get in for anything else.

They laughed.

- Can you play? motioning at the guitar in its case.
- Not really, lied Philippa.

- Elise is here for English, she's a genius, Minnie said proudly. Elise smiled at her.
- I'm doing maths and Annette is here for art history. Minnie was a congenial genius it occurred to her.
- Maths? she echoed.
- And you? Elise asked her. What's your subject?
- English literature or Spanish, Philippa told her.
- Ah, the competition, Minnie said. You'd better go for Spanish or you'll be up against Elise here.
- Not a chance. What about your name? Elise said.
- What about it? Philippa said.
- Is it always Philippa? Elise asked.
- No, it's Phil to my friends, she said.
- How American. A boy's name, Elise sneered.
- Well here it would usually be Pippa.
- Yes Pippa, Minnie supported her.
- Let her be Phil. It's what she wants to…Annette ran out of air unpacking while she spoke.
- Pippa is ridiculous, Philippa said.
- Pippa it is, Elise pronounced her new name and Pippa it would stay at school becoming at times Pip with these friends from school until she left England.

*

They drove in Charles' car to Switzerland. When they had driven high into the mountains of Italy they could see clearly the inscrutable brown rocks and the snow line. It wasn't cold; it was the height of summer and it could easily turn to clouds and rain or snow at any time. In this part of the Swiss Alps you can experience four seasons in one day. It was early morning when they drove into Lausanne to have breakfast. They crossed the Swiss border from Italy with almost no delay. The guards had looked at their passports and had seemed bored, taking the documents inside for only a few minutes to check against the list of passport numbers sought by Interpol recorded in ink in a huge leather book before letting them go. They drove down the mountains toward Lausanne.

It was the time of the jazz festival and they went on to Montreux to the Palace Hotel on the main street that led to the casino. It was bright and sunlit in the white hotel rooms with iron grille balconies looking over the narrow streets with the wide expanse of mountains and blue water in the distance. They closed the long white curtains to be able to sleep in the late morning. When they got up they went out to lunch to eat fresh fried fish and new potatoes.

Montreux was busier than at any other time of the year with the festival in full swing. The streets were filled with throngs of people there for the music festival. Charles and Valerie walked behind Philippa, Christophe and Lorena who seemed to know the way. They walked in the crowd on the esplanade by the lake and then on the main street and then down a side street. They had to forage for a table at the restaurants where there was no favoritism. They went from place to place until they settled in at a table in a charming place, all wood walls, yellow light and white table cloths.

Valerie was annoyed it was not just the three of them in

Switzerland. She felt if she and Charles could just concentrate on talking sense to Philippa it would all be over and they could take her home. Instead Philippa had brought along her friends Lorena and Christophe, the one she knew Charles had met in London. Charles was distracted by Lorena's presence. Lorena was a beautiful blonde indistinguishable from Catherine Deneuve in his view.

- So Christophe, what is it about the festival that draws you? Philippa asked at lunch.
- Yes, and why aren't I surprised to see you here? added Charles amicably.
- I come here every year when I can because it's just incredible! You have the musicians, some of the best jazz players in the world in a place where they feel so relaxed they can just come up to you and talk. Weather Report man! Jaco Pastorius, I hung out with him last year after the show. And the Latin Jazz players--Mongo Santamaria, Ray Barretto, Manu Dibangu, Cecilia Cruz and Tito Puente you are gonna love them! There is no place like Montreux for hanging out with the musicians who like to party and you can spend the whole night with them, as you'll see, just hanging out after the concert and talking and drinking, who knows even playing depending on what's going on. Man! I love it here. Everyone does!

Christophe drank plenty of wine and gesticulated while

he held his rolled cigarettes lit with an expensive lighter from Asprey. He rolled cigarettes constantly throughout the meal with tobacco from a scrolled leather pouch from a London tobacconist while he talked throughout the meal, his genuine enthusiasm winning even Charles over for the meal so that he didn't provoke a fight with him.

Philippa couldn't wait to hear Gato Barbieri though she was excited for Jaco Pastorius in Weather Report in the second set. She rested in the hotel after buying a pair of Spanish alpargatas on the way back to the hotel. They were soft sandals made of canvas soles and black cotton tops with black straps that wrapped around her ankles. She was pleased she had bought them when she dressed for the night of concerts. She wore black Capri trousers and a silver tank top that said **Heaven** in black beads on the back and covered the word with a black cashmere shrug.

Later that night she sat in the back because the sound near the stage was too much and she moved with her counterfeit press pass to the back of the green room where she saw Gato Barbieri the Argentine saxophone player prowling up and down in his white suit and signature Panama hat before he went on.

She wanted so badly to talk to him. She wanted to hear his Argentine Spanish. He was from Rosario in the provinces but he must talk like a porteño from the city she thought. She loved the sound of lunfardo the Buenos Aires slang she had learned to fluency. She wouldn't interrupt him in the trance though. She knew not to do that. He was getting ready to go on. She tried not to look at him. Suddenly he turned his head and looked at her straight on. He looked her in the face, in her eyes.

He seemed to be saying

- Y vos che a vos qué te pasa? Que carajo te pasa?
- What the fuck is up with you?
- What the fuck do you want from me?

Finally he looked away and walked past her and onstage.

She went out front to listen.

She heard that he was and wasn't homesick in his music. He's not devastated to be here! He's like me, he is here and he's doing okay. He's a fish out of water like I am and he's breathing on land. Ha! She looked as he blew the horn under the pink and blue lights in his white suit from under his panama hat tipped but never too low not to see his lips and his face straining She watched him and saw in his face when he played the expression of someone who goes way inside himself to bring his music. He brought the beauty, pity and pain of leaving Argentina with all the emptiness of the Argentine's exile in Europe. He gave his dilemma and distress and joy of the moment filled with amazement to the audience with his playing that night.

Philippa was exhausted. She felt cold, dizzy and short of breath in the casino when he stopped playing. She waited until the last song of the last set when people were clamoring for encores. She knew he would give them. She went outside, lay face and elbows on the lawn of the Montreux Casino and wept. She cried for her city Buenos Aires , how easily she had replaced her with everything British and how she had been callous and shallow to leave her without a second thought, this city that had been a mother to her .

When she had wandered the streets she had never felt afraid in the way she had in London. This was a different fear arising only when she saw the military on the street or the plain clothes men from the secret police in their unmarked green Ford Falcons prowling the streets at night and in the early dawn searching for fresh prey to disappear.

She thought of the way she had often walked the length of Avenida Corrientes on cool nights with her white raincoat wrapped around her carrying her guitar from her classical lessons because her stepfather insisted she walk there and back and it was a very long way.

She liked the walking meditation that took hold after a bit when you noticed the rhythm of the street and were aware of nothing but the act of walking alertly. The streets were endearing. She was fully absorbed in herself and in the moment and didn't compare anything she saw to her home in New York or to anywhere. She accepted wholeheartedly the busy streets packed with pedestrians at times in particular on the big avenues like at the corner of Santa Fe and Pueyrredon where the traffic noise was sickening and the crowds rushed by like winds when the lights changed. She clutched her guitar in its soft case and walked quickly at times slowing down to observe better and when she slowed down she was sometimes woken up out of her awake dreaming. She didn't really hear the men ejaculating in her ear the talk that passes for compliments from men when you walk by in that city.

She lay on the wet grass weeping and thought of the disorder of the crowds, and of the ten lanes of traffic on Nueve de Julio day and night and the sun slanting down onto the Calle Florida where she shopped with her friends in Galeria del Este on Saturday mornings .She saw the cloistered calm of the cafes she liked to sit in with her mother in the afternoon when she could coax her out of the somber townhouse to drink there a Campari and soda . She had loved these somber quiet cafes~ not the modern ones all steel and glass but the old Café Tortoni 's dark wood columns .Waiters in coats served coffee and hot chocolate in thick white cups. She dreamed of the *disquerías* where she could hear any new record from the US before she bought it. Her mother gave her plenty of money to spend so she could move about the city mainly because her mother couldn't calculate the exchange rate of the peso to the dollar in those days.

She thought of the *librerías*, the ones along Avenida Corrientes which stayed open all night .These were her friends the bookstores and how she had stood there for hours reading and thinking one day people would stop there to read her books. There would be a picture of her as the author smiling out from under a black fedora hat.

*

The author's biography on the inside cover would say the following:

Philippa Saenz Peña was born in New York and brought to Argentina at the age of three. She attended the Escuela Normal in Buenos Aires and earned a place at the University of Buenos Aires. She chose instead to emigrate to England where she studied English Literature at Oxford University. After graduating she left England and moved to France and settled in Paris where she resides today. Saenz Peña has been compared to Edith Wharton, Emily Bronte, Luisa Valenzuela, Marguerite Duras, Charlotte Bronte and Virginia Woolf.

*

Lorena rang up Charles

- She's gone, she said.
- Christ, he said. What do you mean?
- She's left. She's in Paris or London, I'm not sure. I woke up this morning and she'd taken her things and her suitcase and the porter saw her leave at dawn in a cab for the airport. She's gone but I think we can catch her.
- How can we when we don't know where she's gone?
- Well, you know the nice man we met last night from America?
- He said he'll get someone to find out for us and in an hour or so we'll know. So get packed and meet me downstairs in an hour.

*

In the early mornings in Buenos Aires you could hear the vendors coming down the street singing the one or two note song and crying as they do in Rome. This was way before the trucks would start flapping down nearby Avenida Santa Fé and on the narrow streets of the Barrio Norte on the uneven tarmac of Arenales and Rodriguez Peña. This was before any lone car came along or the tap of footsteps began or the black and yellow taxis were racing each other madly along Callao.

At this time in the morning the streets were almost silent but for the beginning singing of the cart vendors. None of the shops selling patries were open yet. None of the green metal newsstands selling La Nación, El Clarín, The Buenos Aires Herald, or La Prensa were opened up yet and none of the *kioskos* that sold sweets and school supplies like notebooks which they wrapped in paper and tied up with ribbon or string like precious gifts, were open yet.

There was the *ropavejero* who sold used clothes, the *afilador*, who sharpened knives and scissors, the *verdulero* who had a cart from which he sold vegetables, the *repartidor del almacén* who delivered groceries that you'd order over the phone. Some of them may no longer exist, like the *repartidor*, but from what people tell me, now there are people who go through the trash and pick up recyclables. I believe they're called *cartoneros*.

The strange carts they rolled along in front of them

scraped the cobblestone and tortured the nerves of the early morning sleeper.

The notes of the vendors' voices mixed in with the sounds of the birds. At the back of the house on Juncal in the garden the jacaranda trees swollen with silver threads from the morning sky stood suffering in the warm wind. The smell of jasmine lavender and lily wafted in with the wind along with the city's acrid smell of smoke.

Philippa woke up on Saturday morning with the most intense homesickness for England even though she had only lived there as a child for a year. She dreamed of lush green English gardens and the warm afternoon sun that didn't give you a fever and the cool afternoon rain in London. As it was Saturday she went to find her mother. She found her alone in the dark Chinese den which had red brocade wallpaper and an antique wardrobe and no sunlight as there were no windows.

- Where's papá? She asked anxiously.
- He's gone for the day to buy paintings at galleries.
- When can I leave for England, mummy?
- Oh I don't know dear. You're only thirteen. She took a sip of her scotch and soda.
- School is so easy here mother. I'm not learning anything, she said sternly.
- Well, dear I'll discuss it with your stepfather. You know he doesn't like England.
- But he doesn't like it anywhere, she said.
- That's enough out of you, said her mother stubbing

out another cigarette. You have quite a mouth on you. You should be grateful to him for bringing us here from New York where I would have to worry about you all the time. He can't work because you are all such a problem to us. It's a good thing I have my money for us to live on from my mother or I don't know what we would do. It's your brother who constantly antagonizes him and doesn't respect him as a father. So I don't need any lip from you young lady!

- I'm sorry, I didn't mean to upset you. Calm down.
- You children don't know what you put me through, she said pouring another drink from the decanter.
- Have you had breakfast? Philippa said.
- No, I was too upset. I couldn't sleep.
- Then let me make you something. Then maybe we can go out for a little walk, down Santa Fé. You like Santa Fé. We could even do some shopping for you if you like.
- You'll help me with the shop girls? With my Spanish they're not all so nice I don't understand them and they don't listen to me! They say they speak English but I say I can't understand a word sometimes.
- It's ok. I'll help you. Why don't you get dressed and I'll make us breakfast. Her mother sighed and put out her cigarette.
- It's sure not like New York, she said slurring her words.
- No it's not, Philippa said.

- It's your father's fault, she said tears springing up suddenly, and if it hadn't been for the mess he caused none of this would have happened. If he had left me alone about you kids when I came back nothing would have happened. So I was unfaithful? So I ran off? You kids were fine he had plenty of money to look after you, Dottie saw to that-
- I know mother, she broke in. don't upset yourself about this now. don't think about the past if it's only pain that it brings you.
- Yes, her mother went on, it is upsetting and it is my bad luck. I don't know why I ever had you kids. Nothing has ever gone right for me and you are all trouble. Even you. You can only think of yourself and getting away from us. Just because you are bright and your teachers call you precocious and think you are a genius you think you know what you want. Well if I were you I'd come down from your high horse or get ready for a fall. You think you are ready to go off by yourself to some school in England and you'd be alright there without us? What makes you so sure you can handle that? You're only thirteen years old!

*

Philippa and Christophe were married in city hall in Zurich. Christophe found two alcoholic friends in the famous neighborhood bar in the old city , Zurich Bar frequented by criminals and police alike just like its counterpart next door the night spot Kon Tiki. These two gentlemen in Dickensian rags and roguish artists' clothes who could barely walk to the Rathaus or City Hall stood up with them as witnesses. Then they all went to have breakfast and ordered a bottle of white wine with it even though it was only eight in the morning! Immediately afterwards she stood in line for her identity card and once she had collected it she went right away to the store on the Limmatstrasse to show it to the owner.

- I guess you were true when you said you would have this Swiss papers! he said. You can start tomorrow.

*

They seemed to be driving forever up towards the sky with the motor of the car straining. Her husband Christophe had an expensive car that purred evenly on the steepest slope unlike this car and he was an excellent driver. They drove to Paris and Rome frequently and down to Spain and Morocco.

Music and the music business had become more prominent in their lives and after playing or rehearsing they liked to spend the nights along with everyone else in the business in the Splendid Bar in the old part of the city. There people talked about everything and about the business mainly, how they were doing, who was working with who, who was getting a deal, who had a deal already, who was in New York, who had just come back from New York, and who was going to New York. As a manager Christophe bragged about his acts that were all about to make it big and he would have to go with them immediately to New York.

The Splendid Bar was a very pleasant piano bar open until two a.m. for drinks. It was filled with ubiquitous cigarette smoke and good conversation flowed through the sweet muffled sound of piano music. In this cold city the inhabitants longed for the tropical and for the sun's warmth. The city had a vibrant social life. Zurich was a nightlife city and the party always extended beyond the closing of the bars into someone's house. They often had parties in the apartment. Christophe was an excellent chef and he made great meals taking all afternoon in their confection and requiring huge amounts of wine to be consumed during the entire afternoon's efforts in preparation for the evening. The guests were mainly Swiss and American musicians. One of the Swiss ones, Alex, became a man of interest to Philippa.

She had befriended the Swiss musician at a jazz show in Bazillus, a popular new club in Zurich. Philippa had stopped paying such close attention to the present. It was this silence and a sense of distaste in everything around her that interested Alex about her. He was considered quite the guy around town in the local music world. He was good-looking and slim and liked to wear leather suits, jewelry and long blond hair. He was a percussionist and before he discovered music he had been a bank teller and he liked this life much better with the hours, the women, the pay, the sitting around drinking, smoking and talking.

She noticed herself looking at him when he was talking to other people. He would look at her too. He would walk over to her to her side and she would pretend not to notice.

She would engage purposely in conversation with someone else.

The first time they were alone he wanted to ask her, whatever do you see in that man, other than that he is rich. Instead he said to her, you are very pretty.

- No, I'm not, she replied. But you could say I was interesting.
- Interesting is beautiful, he told her.
- Depends who's looking, wouldn't you say? She smiled and squinted her eyes the way she did at times. She walked away.

The next morning he called her up and invited her to go with him to a recording session later that day.

*

They arrived at the place near Interlaken and went inside the small chalet. The studio was wrapped in Tibetan rugs covering the walls and thick colorful carpet. She sat on the couch to listen.

At one point the electric violinist asked, can you sing at all.?

- I think so.
- Can you just sing a few lines to help us out until the impossibly late Corinne arrives?

He sang the chorus for her.

- It's a simple rock ballad and the lyrics are easy. She sang it. He corrected her.

- Yes, just like that, the violinist said. But over there, in the vocal booth. Don't be scared. We really just need to get the sound the idea even of the singer. It's just the chorus. So, you see?
- Uh –huh, she said and went into the voice booth.
- Okay? She said into the microphone.
- Okay-said the sound engineer. Now just sing a few bars, he told her.

She sang in a whispery voice and then fooled around a bit.

Her voice filled the room even though she made no effort.

- Wow-she said.
- What? said the engineer. He was friendly and had a kind face.
- To sing in a studio-she said
- You've never done it?
- No she said. It's amazing to hear yourself like this.
- Yeah, it's a very good setup, Alex said, great equipment, a great mike and soundboard.
- I think you have an incredible voice, the engineer said smiling at her. I have to turn the levels way down, you don't need it.

- Who knows? We'll see, she said.
- Just listen through the headphones and sing, Alex instructed.
- Just go for it, the violinist said, curious now.

Her voice filled with the song with longing. She blew the words out effortlessly like cigarette smoke. The notes were clear and strong.

They sat silently staring at each other.

- I can't believe how you can sing-said the engineer moving about skillfully in the dark crowded room.

The others in the room all had things to say too.

- Incredible voice! We'll use her on the album.
- I can't believe our luck. Thanks to God the Corinne is late!
- Amazing. Where did you learn to sing like that?

*

- Will you come to my hotel? the engineer asked her when they were standing outside smoking during a break.
- I don't know, she said. She liked his blue eyes, his kind face, his voice, and his obvious intelligence.
- I'm at the Baur au Lac for two more days. After that I have to go back home.
- You're not staying in Europe?

- No. I live in America. I'm here on tour as an engineer. I'm just helping these guys out.
- I'll be there tomorrow afternoon maybe, she said.
- Make it tomorrow morning. We'll have breakfast in the dining room, he said.

*

Christophe didn't like the idea of her having breakfast with the American engineer one bit, or going to the studio with Alex, or singing on the album, or any of the things he was beginning to hear about his wife in Zurich. He wanted men to admire her and he was fiercely possessive and jealous. He threw an expensive trumpet against a wall that night when he came home drunk.

- Fuck, he said. The guy from BMG didn't like the band enough to sign them and you're a whore, he said.

He started to cry and then ripped off his shirt.

- I'm flesh and blood see? he said.
- Yes, I see, she said. All the warm feelings she had ever had drained out of her at that moment and her voice was completely flat.
- How can you treat me this way? I took you out of nothing! You were poor and you were nowhere! I've made you into whatever you are today and you're no great singer! You are nothing, you know.

She tried to walk past him. He took hold of her arm.

He threw her against the wall. She heard a quick snapping sound. He had cracked her ribs. Later, when he had taken her to have them taped he sat in his gray silk suit waiting and smoking and he answered the doctors 'questions without a smirk. He was concerned and frowned for the doctors. He said she had fallen off a horse at his father's place in St. Moritz. She pretended not to understand or speak Swiss German and smiled sweetly while the doctors examined her. That didn't explain to the doctors though why she had waited until getting all the way down from St. Moritz to Zurich to get medical attention.

*

The next morning she waited until Christophe left the apartment and she threw a few pieces of clothing into a bag and took her guitar. She left everything else and packed three notebooks and a book by Gide., The Counterfeiters. She ran three blocks from Gasometerstrasse to Langstrasse where she had the fleeting thought she might be seeing this street of the brothels and the bars for the last time. And that's just fine with me, she thought! Her husband could drown his rage and sorrow as he would there. He always had been a regular customer at the houses along Langstrasse or Long Street in English. She hated this side of him. She got a taxi and took it to the Zurich airport. She was right on time to meet Jesse the engineer.

- I'm so glad you're coming with me, he said.

She took a deep breath. Her body hurt.

- I am too, she said, I am too.

He held her hand when they saw the lights of New York. The city was like the diamond encrusted back of Julia Flyte's turtle in Brideshead Revisited. The city sparkled and beckoned and in between the black lights imploding. She felt fear of the unknown suddenly and had the thought that the change she had made was made now and there would never be anything she could do to undo it. Everything had changed.

She was holding her breath with anxiety. Jesse saw she was paler and shaking suddenly.

- Take a look down there, Jesse said, his eyes reflecting the shiny future. Millions of stars stuck out from the dark blue and black of the earth.
- Don't be afraid, he said. You might just be a star one day...better get used to it.

She laughed and told him You're such an idiot.

- Yeah, I know. But you'll get used to it.
- Welcome home, the woman in uniform said as she walked through to US PASSORTS ONLY.
- Thank you, she said.
- They say that to everyone, Jesse told her.

- Really? she asked. She wondered how she would fit in New York as a porteña from Buenos Aires She didn't feel as if she had returned home. She looked at the large green US passport in her hand with her picture still as a young teenager in Buenos Aires in a starched checked Chanel shirt and long straight brown hair and a smile in the eyes though her mouth was closed. She still felt as if she were absent from her country and from herself.

*

The record company granted her a few days off before the European tour. She would be opening for another band .She was staying at the Hotel Lancaster while she was in Paris. She talked to Lorena to get her to come to the show in Rome.

They met in the green room in Rome while she was warming up. She had waited outside the hotel on the way to the stadium before getting into the van. There was a clear night sky. The moon was a swollen silver spoon.

She met up with Lorena in the green room. She was busy doing laiyaeiyaeiyaeiyaeya with her voice when Lorena arrived with a group of friends. You know, she said, the party is supposed to be after the show. I need to warm up.

- Screw that! Lorena said. I have champagne and all that!
- Afterwards, Philippa said. The room had changed into a party now with people she didn't know

chatting with her band. It looked more like the dressing room of the band they were on tour with who were already a little famous.

People came over to say to her Believe me, I'm not the first person who's going to tell you you're going to be a big star.

- Really, do you think so? Oh that really is so kind of you to say so…Philippa wished she had a dollar for every time she heard herself say words like those that night. She waited for her brother but he never came.
- Lorena, tell me, she said.
- He's been disowned by your family, by his father you know since he last decided to stay.

You've got to talk to him, I think. He can't stay in this state. Charles has left Valerie and has been hanging out in Rome. He says he won't go home until I agree to marry him. I don't know what to do. Of course I feel awful.

She tried to look as if she felt awful but pouting added to her beauty.

- Why don't you marry him?
- Oh I couldn't do that. Lorena shook her long blond hair.
- Will you ever marry anyone? she asked Lorena.

- No, I don't think so, Lorena said shaking her beautiful blond head again.
- Later on she said, Why Charles, Lorena?
- Why anyone, sweetie, Lorena said.

*

They landed at Teterboro airport at around nine pm and drove into New York City on the George Washington Bridge. She wondered why they were taking the Hundred and Twenty-Fifth Street exit to Harlem until they crossed Fifth Avenue and she heard the music coming out of other cars. She recognized her song. She had a feeling of elation and emptiness at the same time. She listened to the sound of her voice and her band mixed in with the sounds of the traffic If you'd heard it, it was a song like any other. The song sounded like any passionate rock ballad filled with a sense of loss and longing.

She opened the roof of the car and stood up. She put her head out to the warm summer air and opened up her voice and she sang the chorus along with the radio into the night air. She put her head back and sang.

Take a good look at yourself
Take a good look at yourself
Take a good look at yourself
Before you look down on me

[illegible]

[illegible] asked. What have you [illegible]
[illegible] the woman said.

*

[illegible] it now?
[illegible] was it?
[illegible] it would.
[illegible]

The Paris Match

Cold Unscaleable Ahead
Lie the Mountains of Instead
From whose cool, cascading streams
None may drink, except in dreams.

~WH Auden

Leila Roberts was very fickle. In the way individuals are, she was very fickle indeed. No sooner had she started one venture, it was often the case, than she dropped it straight away for the sake of another. She was rather beautiful, in a classic way, only she lacked entirely any hint of the confidence that accompanies such young ladies, due to the jealousy of her mother who had told Leila often, at a tender age, that she was not quite pretty but rather attractive, and Leila, having no one with whom to compare this data, had believed her. Not long after Leila's eleventh birthday, the mother up and left, never to be heard from, as she had settled with a film producer in California. This had the effect of saddling Leila with an alcoholic father who hoped the girl would run the house in London for him as smoothly as the mother had, and he kept Leila home from boarding-school sending her instead to private tutors in order that she might take care of him. She had only her father at home and a depressive older brother was allowed his freedom to roam about London as he pleased.

Leila was twenty-two by the time she decided to drop out of London University where she had been wrestling with a degree in Philosophy and Theology against her father's wishes.

- What are you going to be a lifetime student? He badgered.
- No, just until I get my degree.
- Plenty of fine secretarial jobs out there for a girl like you, he would say.

She left London and went to Paris to take up residence with an old school friend by the name of Marguerite who had dropped out of A-Levels tutoring in the first year and rushed to Paris in the wake of an American soldier she wanted to marry. No such luck! On the train to Dover Leila felt like she was dreaming. It wasn't real, it was unusual, staying up all night to pack quietly, writing long letters to her brother and her father, and notes to the housekeeper and secretary she had found for her father. She had decided to stop making decisions. She was going and that was it. She felt compelled to act by something beyond herself. She filled one suitcase with her best clothes and notebooks, a copy of Far From the Madding Crowd for the train. Onboard the boat she stood at the rail and watched England slip away. The sea was gray and turbulent for the crossing and Leila worried about her father. It didn't help the anxious feelings much so she turned her thoughts to Paris and the life she would have there as a writer being among artists and having a life of the mind. She drank a shot of vodka at the bar inside and it steadied her and warmed her inside so that she didn't feel so alone. She thought about Marguerite waiting for her in Paris and the life in front of her according to the prestigious modeling agency she worked for, seemed exciting for a moment. Leila thought how eager she was to hear her friend's story as there was nothing she liked to talk about more than men, women and love.

She took a taxi to the Rue Mouffetard from the Gare de L'Est with a feeling of great excitement in her stomach. It might also have been hunger since she ate nothing on the train from Calais and had no time to stop for coffee at the station. She had rushed out to see the blue of the Paris sky straight away and so had forgotten everything and hailed the nearest taxi.

- Bonjour Monsieur, she said to the driver.
- Bonjour Mademoiselle, vous allez ou?
- Rue Mouffetard, Numero 105.
- Vous savez que aujourd hui c'est la marché la ?
- Non, je ne savais pas. Ca me fait pas difference.
- Ah oui, mais il faudra que vous marchez!

She had smoked a number of cigarettes since early that morning. She felt dizzy and nauseated but she thought about her friend Marguerite. Her friend she knew was waiting excitedly to see her. There would be breakfast or they would make breakfast together.

It was the day of the open air market as the cab driver had told her and as it was impossible for the driver to go up the street, she got out several houses before, and walked with the suitcase in which she had put everything she held dear and for Marguerite some presents she had picked with care. The door of Number 105 was not easily seen. She went past it once and had to ask someone. Finally she found it, an entrance portal painted an ugly green with the faint digits faded above. She went inside and found herself in a Moorish courtyard where the open air surprised her. She had no idea where to go. There appeared no exits or entrances except the heavy wooden door back to the street.

She stood in the courtyard and shouted

- Marguerite! Marguerite, where are you?

She repeated this. It was obvious no one was waiting for her.

A resident replied crankily to her shouting.

- What do you want? An old woman yelled, for God's sake down there! You don't have to shout!
- For the love of God what is it, another voice joined in.
- I'm sorry. I'm looking for my friend Marguerite, a young girl with blonde hair.
- She is on the second floor. Take the stair.

- Where is it? I mean the stair?
- There, there, to your left. Young people. You don't look anymore.
- I see, thank you, Leila said.
- Young people! another voice said, in a parting shot.
- Thank you, Leila said to no one in particular.

She climbed the crumbling circular stair the residents had indicated. She though it odd that the noise had not disturbed Marguerite. She got to the second floor and knocked on the door. There was no sound of movement inside. She knocked loudly and called again to her friend, Marguerite, it's me. I'm here! Marguerite! Open Up!

She heard something like a moan and after that the sound of movement and then the sound of the locks being withdrawn. There stood Marguerite in a long white nightgown in the middle of the morning looking as if she had been pulled up from the deepest sleep imagined. She was at this moment yawning and starting to try to smile at her friend.

Baby, she said in a muffled tobacco ravaged voice murmuring to Leila, well, do come in.

Leila went in.

The place was not bright, in fact it was hard to see at first as the light was dim. There was a dark green carpet that covered the crooked old floorboards. The room seemed to be at a tilt and the ceiling curved. There was a closet of a kitchen with a cutout in the wall which went through to the sitting- room, bedroom. A table and two chairs stood against one wall. A window gave onto the street and a double bed took up most of the room. There was a niche in the wall by the table for the telephone, which Leila noticed with pleasure. She loved to use the telephone. A bathroom with Spanish tile floor completed the flat.

- How much are we paying for this place? asked Leila, always quite concerned with money.
- A thousand dollars a month? I know it's a lot but it's so hard to find anywhere really so once I got my job I couldn't be bothered to look. I got it from a man at the American School. Do you like it?
- Well, no, not really. For a thousand dollars…
- No, I didn't think you would, said Marguerite.
- And it's much too much! We'll have to change soon. Anyway, now that I'm here

I can go out to look.

- Yes, well, it's hard, I told you, said Marguerite as she went into the cutout of a kitchen to make tea.

When they sat down together Leila noticed how tired and worn-out her friend looked. Marguerite had great blue circles under her eyes and her skin was washed with pale gray. Paris must be hard on her! Leila thought, and she tried not to tire Marguerite with lots of questions.

Marguerite seemed lively despite her appearance and the arrival of her friend had put her very much in the mood for talk. She told Leila all about her life so far in Paris. She talked about her job as a house model in the Rue St. Denis and how she spent her days there trying on clothes for clients who admired her and going out in the evenings to restaurants and cafes, and after so little time she knew Paris pretty well she boasted. She promised to show Leila around and assured her she would love the city as much as she did. Her American soldier had abandoned her straight away she told Leila. When she came to see him on arriving in Paris he had not only wanted nothing more to do with her after leaving London but he left for America the very next week.

- I'm worried about getting work. I can't work legally here, Leila said.
- Don't worry, I'll help you there. In fashion you don't need papers. In anything really. Don't worry.
- Yes, but I'm not a model getting bookings like you and I don't know how to do anything useful.
- Don't worry, baby, Marguerite said, we'll talk later, and as for that evening they would go to visit Marguerite's mother who lived in a nice flat in the Rue Notre Dame, luxurious by comparison. From there you could see the church and at night it was beautiful.

Being English, Marguerite and her mother could work legally in France with no problem. Marguerite's mother worked as a travel agent. Leila had met her in London.

Leila wanted to rest from her long train journey and as for the afternoon they slept. They were both too tired to go out and in between her dreams Leila woke up thinking clearly about her plans for work. There would be jobs she could get and it would be harder than having British papers she knew. The one connection she kept with her mother was having chosen American citizenship at the age of twenty-one. She had never been to America and she prized the big green passport, keeping it wrapped in a soft leather case. She would often take it out of its case, feel the grain of the green cover, look at the black and white photograph on the inside of a girl with long dark hair and pale skin, and turn the pages looking at the stamps. She had found it amusing and odd when the French Customs officer on the train as they left Calais for Paris had looked at her passport and said as if he did not believe her.

- Vous êtes Americaine ?
- Oui, Monsieur .Je suis Americaine. Yes, Sir. I am American.

She did not know what that really meant, she was finding out.

It was 1982 and Paris was on edge and there was tension in the wind after France had been brutalized by terrorists for decades and there was the ever escalating violence.

Marguerite showed Leila how she liked to walk the streets. She and Leila were prone to the profession. This was what she meant when she said don't worry, you won't need working papers here, it's easy. Marguerite was very good at it and she got Leila to copy her. Marguerite loaned her clothes to Leila until she could afford her own. They dressed well out of habit as well as reason and they looked striking crossing the boulevards in their high silver boots the light catching the shiny clips in their hair.

- Sure beats going home, doesn't it? Marguerite would say whenever she saw that pensive look of Leila's appear.
- I guess, Leila would reply.

As soon as she saw the opportunity Marguerite took Leila to a café on the Place de la Contrescarpe where they met a few businessmen. Afterwards they went to a hotel. They went often to the hotels after that, trying to be careful not to get hurt and watching out for each other. Marguerite and Leila took turns waiting for each other downstairs when they went to the hotels.

They worked in the hotel bars sometimes when the bartender was friendly to a large tip to let them sit there at the bar. This would only happen if no one else was working in the bar at that moment , though if things didn't happen quickly they would leave soon so the hotel wouldn't report them to the local police and gangsters .They wanted to be independent and were playing about on the edges of a very established business with its own harsh set of rules.

They used to go in the afternoon to a neighborhood café near The Sorbonne and one day Leila noticed the paper the man sitting next to her held. The characters were unfamiliar to her and the script strange to her with its curls and dots.

She noticed the direction from which he was reading wasn't from left to right and she found herself staring at the page over his shoulder. His hair was dark blonde and his hands a shade of green. He looked at her and said, Something different, huh? Arabic.

- Not what I can read, I'm afraid, she said.
- Ah, but you speak French and English with your friend.
- Yes, badly.
- French or English? He laughed after he said this.
- Both probably, she said, smiling.

Marguerite told her the paper was in Arabic, the guy was a student from the Middle East, and she had found him good-looking. He looked to her, Marguerite said, as if he had plenty of money and could be a good prospect for her. She said usually he was surrounded at table by a bunch of friends.

- You know, a good ride, Marguerite told her.
- I'm not looking for a good ride, Leila told her.
- Well, I am. That's for sure, sweetie. So, hands off Omar.
- I haven't got my hands on, said Leila.
- No, that's true, Marguerite agreed with her. He probably just wants to get to me by chatting you up first, she said.

Marguerite was confident and not apologetic of her own power and she was definitely a Deneuvesque beauty with blonde hair, green eyes, a round face, an easy laugh, an alto voice, and a beautiful body though not tall enough to walk in runway shows. Besides. There was no modeling work for them in Paris, runway, print or otherwise. At least not for Leila and even Marguerite had long ago given up looking.

*

Soon they would see Omar in there every day as they went in for a cup of tea. Sometimes Marguerite would start to drink in the afternoon. Leila never drank. Marguerite was dressed up in designer clothes and high heels, attracting a lot of attention. Leila was dressed simply in black. They shared a table with him always and Marguerite flirted tirelessly. Omar liked Leila. Leila was never too alert at these meetings, being a night owl. She had a belief that the more important things take place later in the afternoon, evening and night, and that nothing that was happening to her now was of any real importance. She had an intuition she had to forget herself and forget life in order to live it. She paid her surroundings very little attention at times. She seemed distant and aloof which annoyed people at times. Omar liked her lack of conversation. She never said anything to him unless he spoke to her. They exchanged looks. They stopped in at the café in the afternoons and in the evenings for a coffee on their way to the tourist bars and to the hotels.

- Why say anything? Why do anything? Her eyes seemed to say.

Meanwhile Marguerite chattered on.

*

Omar was a doctoral student of Political Science at the Sorbonne. He asked Leila if she would like to attend a lecture with him.

- No, I don't think Marguerite would like that, she said.

She found she was thinking of him. She dreamed she said to him I'm a hypocrite.

We are all hypocrites, he replied.

- I'm a prostitute.
- I'm a prostitute too, he said. We all are.

*

She had doubts about what she was doing in Paris and she did not allow herself to indulge in much introspection. She had lost her family. They had betrayed her. God had betrayed her. She had been a Catholic and now she never set foot in a church. She was alone in the world and she could not see that she was lost. He gave her a Cartier diamond and sapphire bracelet. It must have cost 200,000 francs. She hid it.

*

Once Leila called her father. He had relocated to New York for the winter.

- Hello Daddy, I'm fine.
- What are you doing?
- I'm studying, she lied.
- Studying what? He asked.
- French and mime, she lied.
- Hmm. And who's paying for it?
- Oh, they are…her voice sank.
- They? He asked. She'd already hung up.

He was drinking heavily all night while he sat with her. He did not want to get up.

When Marguerite went over to the bar, Omar leaned over and said in Leila's ear,

- Would you like to come with me to eat little cakes at a patisserie I know tomorrow?
- I will get you with my car at three.
- Alright, said Leila.

*

She did not tell Marguerite. She said she did not feel well

and would not work that afternoon. He said she would rest and work later in the evening. Marguerite went shopping. Leila liked nothing better than to visit a good patisserie. He collected her in a black car with a driver. They went several times and Omar seemed to glance out the window at a restaurant across the street. She wore the bracelet he gave her and forgot to take it off before she returned home. Marguerite saw it.

- Be careful, she said.

*

It was August and it was hot and the shutters were closed to keep the cool inside. Leila was hearing the news on the radio about the bombing in the Rue des Rosiers. She remembered he had focused his attention on the restaurant across the street.The Restaurant Jo Goldenberg had been ravaged by two men who threw grenades inside. The place was in the Jewish quarter of Paris Le Marais. The radio announcer mentioned terrorist attack. People had been killed and gravely injured.

*

The time was half past four and he hadn't come for her yet. Maybe he had something better to do. She was anxious. The phone rang and he spoke to her in a tense voice.

- I can't come today. I have to go away. I'm in trouble.

Leila listened.

- I did some things I believe in and now I am in trouble and it's time to go.
- I see.
- Do you forgive me Leila?
- I do not agree with your actions. I think you are a misled man, Omar.

-----Leila. I will come back. Okay.

- Okay, Omar.

*

Marguerite brought the evening papers.

Two assailants throw grenades into the dining room of the Chez Jo Goldenberg restaurant and fire machine guns at the patrons. Six people die, including two American tourists, and 22 others are wounded in the attack on the Jewish restaurant in Paris's Marais district.

The Chez Jo Goldenberg restaurant attack on the Rue des Rosiers in Paris, was attributed to the Abu Nidal Organization

She lay in bed paralyzed with fear. What had she done? Nothing, she told herself. Who was Omar? A monster?

A person so dead inside that human life meant nothing to him or someone who thinks they have the truth…

How could she not have known? She knew only one side

of him. She could not cry. She was too afraid. She had no one to go to, no one to call, no family really, as they had abandoned her in Europe. She would need a lawyer. She could not call the embassy as they would call her father. What were they going to charge her with? Eating cakes with a man she didn't know was a terrorist.

*

The police came at seven in the morning. They were polite.

She tried not to shake when she opened the door.

- Questions? She said.
- Questions, said the detective.

She was already dressed and set to go with them.

Once in the office of the Prefecture, they were not polite.

- You are an American prostitute who frequents Islamist terrorists.
- Do I have it right? The detective asked her.
- I am an American working fashion model with a lot of friends. Men. Male friends.
- Yes, we see that Miss Roberts.
- I am often in the company of men; Marguerite and I are both models…
- You work in the hotel bars, you have been seen at The Ritz and The Relais Plaza as well as other places.

- Well we can't work legally here, and I have nowhere else to go.
- Nowhere else to go? We know you are the daughter of the wealthy American oil man Rex King..
- I have nowhere to go.
- So a rich girl, playing about with danger in Europe. Are you a terrorist sympathizer?
- No, no sir I am not. She did not flinch when she answered.

Everything was going to work against her. She was about to give in to vertigo. She gripped the table to steady herself. Her vision blurred. She gripped harder.

- Ne touchez pas la table, a guard said. Ne touchez pas la table, Mademoiselle.

She fell on the floor and lost consciousness.

*

There is a lengthy history of terrorism in France, reaching back to the beginning of the twentieth century. In 1914, at the outbreak of World War I there was the assassination of Jean Jaurès a socialist leader and a committed antimilitarist, in a Parisian cafe, by French nationalist Raoul Villain. There was the shooting of Symon Petliura in Paris on the Rue Racine, by a Russian revolutionary Sholom Schwartzbard in 1926. There was a bomb attack by La Cagoule against the Union des Industries et Métiers de la Métallurgie and the

Confédération Générale du Patronat Français to create the impression of a communist conspiracy, and an unsuccessful attempt by National Liberation Front, Algeria to assassinate the French Information Minister Jacques Soustelle on the Place de l'Etoile in Paris. 1961 brought the Vitry-Le-François train bombing carried out by the Organisation Armée Secrète, which caused a fast Strasbourg–Paris train to derail; the worst terrorist attack in French history before the 21st century. A bomb attack was carried out on the Quai d'Orsay, by the OAS, and the OAS launched a car bomb attack in Issy-les-Moulineaux. There was a bomb attack against the Algerian Consulate in Marseille by the far-right Charles Martel Group, a bomb attack against the Spanish Consulate in Toulouse by Revolutionary Internationalist Action Groups, and a grenade attack on the Drugstore Saint-Germain-des-Prés, allegedly by Carlos the Jackal.

In the years leading up to the bombing in the Rue des Rosiers there were two failed rocket propelled grenade attacks on El Al airplanes at Orly Airport by Carlos the Jackal . There was the Black September Bomb attack in the Gare de l'Est. Hostages were taken at the Iraqi embassy in Paris, by the Palestine Liberation Organization, PLO. Three terrorists opened fire on El Al passengers at Orly Airport while they waited in the departure lounge. There was the assassination of the PLO representative in Paris, Izz al-Din al-Kalak and one of his assistants, by the Abu Nidal Organization. There was a bomb attack against a university restaurant in a Jewish student hostel in Paris claimed by an Anti-Zionist group. The Turkish attaché for tourism in France, Yılmaz Çolpan was assassinated on the Champs Elysées by the JCAG, and the director of the Palestinian library-shop in Paris, Yusef Mubarak, was assassinated by the Abu Nidal Organization.

There had been a bomb attack against the Syrian Embassy in Paris, a bomb attack in the west terminal of Orly Airport, claimed by the far-left group Action Directe. The former Prime Minister of Syria, Salah al-Bitar was assassinated in his newspaper office in Paris. In 1980 there was a Turkish Consulate attack in Lyon, carried out by the Armenian Secret Army for the Liberation of Armenia, known as ASALA .

In 1980 there was a Paris synagogue bombing of the French Israeli Liberal Union on the Rue Copernic. There was the assassination of the Turkish Labour Attaché, Reşat Moralı, and the Religious Affairs Officer in the Turkish Embassy, Tecelli Arı by two gunmen from ASALA in Paris. Bomb attacks were carried out at Ajaccio airport shortly after the arrival of French President Valéry Giscard d'Estaing. And by a Palestinian group in the Intercontinental Hotel in Paris.

In 1981 ASALA attacked the Turkish Consulate in Paris .The United States Assistant Army Attaché Charles R. Ray, was assassinated by the Lebanese Armed Revolutionary Faction. A bomb attack against the Capitole train between Paris and Toulouse, was attributed to Carlos the Jackal. An assassination of an Israeli embassy advisor Yaacov Barsimentov in Paris was carried out, claimed by the Lebanese Armed Revolutionary Faction. A car bomb attack outside the Parisian offices of anti-Syrian newspaper *Al-Watan Al-Arabi*, was attributed to Carlos the Jackal. A bomb attack in a terrace café on the Place Saint-Michel in Paris, was carried out by ASALA.

The Goldenberg restaurant attack on the Rue des Rosiers in Paris, was attributed to the Abu Nidal Organization

*

They questioned her for twenty-four hours. She drank coffee and smoked. She never tired.

Fear kept her wide awake.

- Your friend, Marguerite de Vesey, has told us you knew you worked for Omar Abdullah and that you handed her the money to give to him for protection every night in the café.

She thought quickly. It had never once crossed her mind that the working had begun other than randomly, because they needed cash. She knew immediately that she had been recruited and Marguerite had been playing a game pretending she was a novice. She knew she was going to drown. No one would believe her.

- This man Omar Abdullah, did he ever mention the name Abu Nidal to you?
- No he did not.
- Did you meet any of his colleagues other than at the café?
- No, I did not.

- We will not take you into custody, Miss Roberts. You are free to go.
- Sorry?
- No. We have already established your friend did not tell the truth and that you came to Paris as a model for an agency and fell into bad ways. You are not connected with these people. Your father has heard of the matter and has retained an attorney on your behalf. Avocat Francois Duhot. He is waiting outside for you. He will drive you to the airport. You will both leave for America immediately. In the event that anything changes Avocat Duhot will inform you so that he may accompany you on your return to Paris. I had only the two questions to ask you.
- Thank you.
- Thank you for your time and good luck, said the Inspector. He shook her hand.
- Go home. It's not a life for you, he added, Look to the company you keep.
- Thank you, Sir. Thank you very much.
- Downstairs and outside she slipped into the back seat of the black car beside Monsieur Duhot.

She watched Paris slide past and away all the way to the airport. By the time the plane took off, she could hardly remember why she'd ever longed to come to Paris at all.

*

[illegible] The [illegible]

[illegible] And [illegible] this [illegible]
[illegible] to go [illegible]

[illegible] down [illegible]
[illegible] and [illegible]
[illegible] and [illegible]
[illegible] with the [illegible]
[illegible] and [illegible]
[illegible] I [illegible]
[illegible]

*

Put Your Hands Where I Can See Them

> If you should see a man coming towards you with the intention of doing you good--run for your life..
>
> Henry David Thoreau

The judge was late that morning. Four hours late. The federal attorneys milling about in her courtroom discussed her habitual tardiness. She was known to do things like go to the hair salon. When she arrived at one in the afternoon her hair looked very nice in fact. Clients and their lawyers sat and waited in the federal courtroom, the Supreme Court of the Southern District of New York, for sentencing. There were four cases on that day. There were two routine bank teller theft cases, the sentencing of an important international drug dealer, and there was the bank fraud case that was mine.

I had stood in front of this judge before when I pled guilty to a federal misdemeanor for bank fraud.

The night before I pled guilty I memorized the plea I was to make, and I practiced saying it over and over again. Like a novena. When I most needed it, I had forgotten how to pray.

Then came the year of waiting. I would wait a year for sentencing. I threw myself into my work interpreting and advocating for immigrants at a major city hospital, I savored moments with my family and friends, and I visited my pre-trial probation officer once a month. I was terrified. I had unassailable insomnia. I knew I was going to prison and there was no way out of that. Everyone told me the opposite. I tried to find ways to get stronger in mind and body for what was inevitable.

I started meditating with one exercise, tonglen, a sending and receiving meditation I had learned reading books by Tibetan Buddhists. My breath was all I had control of and it calmed me

*

Four years before I left my Buddhism class with Dr. Robert Thurman at Barnard and went to pick up my voice mail messages as we did in those days from the payphone.

I used a phone card to make the call to a local number, using a service called Ansaphone. My manager had gone to pay for my post office box at Rockefeller Center. I was calling to find out where we would meet.

There were three messages. The first one said.

"Hello, Uncle Sy, I'm down here with the FBI."

The second went into details. The third said the FBI was taking him downtown and that a lawyer should call and come there –always keeping up the pretext these messages were not for me—and that they would be questioning him. He mentioned a name of an agent the lawyer should use when calling in.

I was on the Columbia campus and I headed out to the

subway on Amsterdam Avenue. I took the train to fifty-seventh street and then went to a payphone. I asked for Agent Davis.

- It's her, she said and handed over the phone to a man.
- This is Agent Vic Bellini of the Federal Bureau of Investigation. You are wanted for bank fraud.
- You should go to the nearest police station and turn yourself in.
- So this is the best my family can do? So you work for my family now? So this is perfect.

I screamed at him. I had not learned to remain calm. I was twenty –nine. I knew I had plenty to worry about though I did not know exactly what, and bank fraud had never occurred to me.

Agent Bellini held the phone up in the air so people in the room could hear me shouting at him.

- Do you hear her? Can you hear her? She's a drug addict. She's high on drugs!

This confirmed for me my family's involvement with the FBI and this situation. Only they would talk about my taking drugs. I had divorced my physically and emotionally abusive Swiss narcotics trafficker husband in Zurich and moved to New York at the age of twenty-one, everyone knew me as a hard working singer who never smoked or drank alcohol and worked constantly writing and recording music. Everyone knew I ran from voice class to dance class to yoga and to volunteer at God's Love We Deliver. I had left the world of day jobs, law firms and courtrooms since hooking up with manager man Joe Miller.

Some nights I hung out with my friends who were musicians and I went to watch the dancers at El Barrio when there was Salsa. I was older than the pre-requisite twenty – three to become a rock star and I did not take drugs. I was obsessed with success and financial independence as well as emotional independence from my family. I was with a man I did not like, who frightened me, because of my ignorance of the music industry.

- You need to turn yourself in right now. Agent Bellini said.

He went on - There is a warrant for your arrest. We have been investigating you for six months.

- If I turn myself in will you let him go
- We don't negotiate. The FBI does not negotiate with you. What's so special about this guy that you want us to let him go?

It had been two minutes and ten seconds. I hung up the phone.

I went down into the subway and as I ran down the stairs,

I changed my coat for another in my dance bag. I went up the opposite stairs back onto 57th street and I called him again.

- I had no idea you were investigating me.
- Well, normally when the FBI investigates people we don't tell them.
- Will you let him go if I come in?
- Who is this guy to you that you would turn yourself in for him? Is he in this too?
- No, we do not make deals with you. No. He stays
- Then no deal. I am not turning myself in. I don't care.

After that conversation, my life changed forever. I became an immigrant in my home country. Years later this same FBI agent, a very fine agent who dedicated himself to anti-terrorism well before September 11th, would shake my hand and say, I'm sorry for your troubles.

He was released the following day. I heard this voicemail on the payphone in the lobby of the Martha Washington Hotel where I had taken a room, and I would have to wait for another opportunity to talk to him. He sounded cheerful, he said.

- Hey everybody I'm out and I'm fine, so don't worry.

Since the number was meant to be private to the two of us I wondered who everybody was and who else was leaving him messages?

I spent the day sitting upright on my bed in my dreary room listening to a woman weeping somewhere. I had paid for phone service so I called my father's fiancé who was an attorney, She said I should call my mother and everything would be straightened out as soon as I told them where I was.

I thanked her for talking. There was no reason to call my mother unless I wanted to be arrested.

I was not sure of the crime, though I had witnessed and been made to take part in financial fraud and other crimes ever since I had hooked up with Joe Miller. In my ignorance none of it seemed worthy of the FBI.

My plan was to find a room and work. Disappear into the city and hire an attorney. I had read Sun -Tsu and I remembered when your enemy is stronger than you retreat and gain strength first. I retreated.

*

I had also helped my father transfer half a million dollars in funds when he was about to be prosecuted by the IRS and charged with embezzlement by the criminal court. I did not know the indictments were coming for sure though I guessed. He used my German language skills to call a man in Europe to move the money. I thought this was the problem. Otherwise why would they have let Joe go ? He was a career criminal and he found a mark when he met me.

One day when my father hit me with his fist and it caught me in the eye and sent me reeling against the wall, I woke up hours later to find him packing to go to Virginia to look at horses.

He had no recollection of what had happened as he had sobered up somewhat at the prospect of his trip to Williamsburg, Virginia on horse business. We lived in a townhouse on the Upper East Side, on Seventy-Third Street between Madison and Park.

I paid the bills, four thousand for rent, two thousand to The Post House for meals and Liquor, Fifteen hundred to The Regency Hotel Bar, eight hundred for electricity, one thousand for groceries, one thousand two hundred for London Town Car. The list went on.

I went to find my friends on Sixth Avenue, the working girls in fur coats. I wanted to hear more about the trade again. I would invite them for breakfast at The Wellington. Maybe it was time to get in.

The sex business' presence is ubiquitous in the city. I knew young women who said they worked in it. There were brokers at Wall Street firms who worked for escort agencies at night to enhance their salaries, actresses who had to pay rent, models that weren't getting bookings, shop girls who earned almost nothing at fine establishments, and local waifs who had nothing better to do. It had never interested me. The money always sounded ridiculous and the whole thing should have seemed easy enough. Not for me. You can't touch me if I don't love you. I don't care who you are and I've already run through millionaire husbands I thought I loved and not taken a penny. My freedom was all I wanted! Independence from my family was what I craved and yet I was clueless taking care of an active alcoholic with Korsakov's Syndrome who had never been a father to me.

When it comes to the sex trade, lucrative as it can be. I could not get past that moment, where the money is given and the permission granted. I was not meant for this transactional role. I never cared about being an exclusive escort where I never see the check you gave my manager and I just need a bag and a passport for the weekend. I knew this immediately when I met escort agency owner Joe Miller real name Weissman and he started telling me about the business. He would tell me how much money the women made, how they could afford designer clothes, bags and shoes, jewelry, entrance into the best restaurants, and were driven in black Mercedes sedans about town. I was not interested in clothes. I cared about being a recording artist with a legacy, and a role model to young women. And immortality. What does Arthur Miller say an artist wants? We are writing our name in a cake of ice on a hot day, and we want it to be stone.

At the age of twenty-seven I was a hopeless romantic. I thought the gallery owner who lived in Tribeca and called me to hang out once in a while was in love with me. Later I figured out he thought I was wealthy.

I worked as a model and it did not seem sustainable suddenly. I was not really tall enough and I did not enjoy the lifestyle. I wanted to do something that mattered. My father's need for a steady high income was a serious burden for me. No one in the family wanted to help and he seemed to have no friends. No one except creditors called the house. I did not know he talked to his brother and a female friend when I was out. I was alone in the situation and he was a fierce alcoholic in mental and physical decline. No one cared. I recalled his generosity to other people in the past and how he had helped friends in distress. I did not want him to become ill and he was in a weakened state, while he was increasing his intake of alcohol.

I started as a tour guide at the UN. The pay was so low I was afraid to come home. I was desperate to find a second job when I discovered the criminal court downtown. I got hired on the spot as a Spanish language court interpreter and got paid very well.

There was no way I could pay for my father's expenses on my language salary from the courts.

One day I went to the newsstand at Fifty-Seventh and Sixth Avenue and bought an issue of Variety and an edition of Showtime. The trades have escort agency ads in the later pages. I called and made an appointment to meet Joe Miller as he answered his phone and the other numbers I called were busy. What bad luck!

I wrote out a check for my father and a note saying he could count on me and I was gone.

We met in a coffee shop and I never went back to my father's house. No one looked for me either.

I may have told you, I have no family.

My mother took us to Argentina during the time of The Dirty War. My grandfather died less than a year later. We had abandoned him.

All I know is that after twenty-two hours of flying from Argentina we landed in England when I was sixteen, and in England it was raining, and we had to wait a while on the runway at Heathrow to disembark. It was pitch black out, and pouring at three in the afternoon, and the steel stairs were treacherous. It was raining heavily. I got down on my knees and kissed the tarmac. In the land of Habeus Corpus!

I have never worked in the sex trade and it was not my intention to work as an escort when I met Joe Miller. I wanted to work in the back office and handle the phones. I wanted to understand the business and make the contacts that would lead to my recording contract eventually.

That was the overarching plan. Except Joe Miller had no agency and his finances were in ruins. He was a grifter. Not only did I work the back office –you name the company I answered the phone in that name—I played major roles in his scams. He could not have done them without me. He was not actually that bright. He made mistakes that made us have to leave town in the middle of the night like forging a lease for the electric company to turn the lights back on.

One morning he asked me to dress really well and get ready to go to the bank. He said I should use a British accent and the second name on the account Hannah Miller. He was taking advantage of banking check clearing policies to withdraw money before a check has cleared and there appears to be money in the account. Two days earlier he had asked me to deposit a ten thousand dollar check into that account. It crossed my mind the money might not be there. I didn't ask questions. I got ready and into character of an upper class British graduate student at Columbia for the year. We went to the bank on Broadway around the corner from the Columbia campus. At the bank I spoke to the manager and had to work hard to persuade him to let me withdraw ten thousand dollars from a new account with funds based on a check that hadn't really cleared. It was accomplished using a lot of charm. I walked out with the money. As I couldn't verify the charges, I thought maybe this is what Agent Bellini had in mind for Bank Fraud.

We stayed at The Gramercy Park Hotel for two nights where no ID was required, and where I was so tired I checked in as Kate Moss. No one noticed. We knew there was no alternative to running, and then we left New York City. We drove north to Boston. Once we were having tea during a break in Hartford, and the tears escaped and started rolling down my face silently.

- Don't do that. He said. You'll draw attention to yourself.

When I went on the run I knew I would never see my friends again, that life as I knew it was gone.

One of my good friends had counseled me to wait for the FBI to turn up and let them take me in. She pointed out that this is the USA and not Argentina where we grew up and they would abide by the law in handling my custody. She touched a nerve as I was aware of growing up in a country that abuses authority and which is known for the sad introduction of the word disappeared as a noun into the language and common nomenclature.

- They will just arrest you and take you in. They will

not mistreat you. You are in the United States said my friend an attorney, Miriam on the phone from London.

- Right. Right. Thank you. You've been a real friend. I'll let you know…

We had shared a room in the pension house near school as teenagers as it was safer than traveling from the city to its suburbs every day. My parents soon moved to a far-off province and life at the villa so I had no adult supervision, except my headmistress. How could Miriam say that, just let them take you? They had seen the tanks roll by and the helicopter that took Isabelita Perón to Bariloche together from the balcony the night of the military coup. The Señora who ran the pension rushed to pull them off the balcony pleading Girls, the soldiers, get out of sight!

I saw myself handcuffed to a bed with the word LIGA written in blood above on the wall.

I started destroying all of Joe's files so I could run.

*

Disappearing had been going on for some years and it was after the Military ratified the Statute for the Process of National Reorganization that the mythical dirty war really began. The government now the Junta had issued its own license to kill while masking their crimes with the fictive war on the state by terrorists.

People--not only and generally young people-- began to disappear off the streets, from their way to their jobs and from their homes at night. Disappearances were carried out by squads of men in plain clothes as they cruised the streets of Buenos Aires in the night and early dawn stalking their designated prey and taking into their net anyone who might have the bad luck to be caught. Sometimes, bored junior officers said years later, they just looked for young attractive women they might take back to The Naval School to rape, torture and kill. These gangs drove green Ford Falcons without license plates, into which the victim was placed hooded into the trunk usually having been beaten first. The citizens of Buenos Aires began to disappear in great numbers. Most of them were never seen again.

When in desperation parents or relatives sought information as to the whereabouts of the victims they were told by the police and the military that the authorities had no knowledge of who had taken the victim or where the victim was.

When lawyers were retained to go forward and to bring habeus corpus actions these motions and cases were usually dismissed out of hand by the courts and by military appointed judges. Many judges feared the military regime and had no authority to question the military's denials of knowledge about the victims' disappearances. Some lawyers who brought forward motions of habeus corpus began to disappear as well as their clients. Judges sympathetic to the cause had to go into hiding when they went home and move frequently. They were threatened and menaced and sometimes assassinated in the street.

Meanwhile the military junta played out the farce that

they were waging war on terrorism when the state were in fact the terrorists at this time in Argentine history.

*

The drug dealer kept pacing up and down in his well-cut colorful suit, followed by his posse of men in suits. I would be sentenced first. The bank tellers had been given a free pass and probation.

I was really uneasy. My attorney said things looked good. I did not share his confidence.

I was positive the promise of no prison time for my cooperation would not hold. No one can control the judge, in the end, my lawyer kept saying. The prosecutor, the Assistant US Attorney and my attorney were huddled at the bench in what became a loud argument with the judge.

*

There was another time I had been to the bank near Columbia where we lived. He had an enormous old prewar apartment he had been granted as a graduate student, though he had never been a student at the university. They were always trying to evict him and he went to court and got continuances and continued to live for free. It was a rambling dark place with two balconies that gave out onto at the end of the street the Cathedral of St. John the Divine. He had painted the windows over in black purportedly to discourage break ins from the scaffolding platform outside the windows.

He wrote me a check for ten thousand dollars for the

money he owed me and it was double the amount. He told me to deposit it in my personal account at Chase Manhattan Bank in Rockefeller Center. The following morning he told me to get dressed as I was going to the bank on our behalf to withdraw the money. There was a local Chase branch and he wanted me to insist to the Manager and not come out without the cash. He waited across the street at a coffee shop.

I wore a black Dior suit, a white Yves Saint Laurent blouse, Stephane Kélian boots and carried a Prada bag over one arm, clutching a pair of leather gloves. I put a lot of rouge on, so as not to appear so pale. I practiced a British accent. We decided on the pretext, that I needed to pay tuition today for the start of Fall Semester. I intuited that what Manager Man was doing was taking advantage of vulnerability in the check clearing process where the funds may appear to be available when in fact they are not.

The check was written in the name of Miles Standish-Jones. It was an alias and he had many and I wondered if the money was really there and why he wanted me to withdraw it now. I asked him why and he yelled that of course the money was there and it was just convenient to take it out. To move it from account to account. How so? I asked. It seemed like this was a regular practice in his business.

For safety purposes, he said grimly. After that, I didn't press.

I imagined it must be hard work to be a criminal and move money around all the time. I just had the one bank account, often overdrawn.

*

When I wasn't dressing up to impress bank managers, I was wearing designer clothes and eight inch heels from Madison Avenue designer boutiques. He got hold of these items using fake credit cards and other methods. I was happy in jeans and sneakers and I felt self-conscious walking down the street with him dressed this way and calling a lot of attention to myself.

He insisted on strong makeup and that was against my taste as well. Working as a fashion model had made me enjoy clean skin and simple clothes. My friends at school would have called me All Tarted Up. I got way more attention from men than I wanted.

*

We quarreled in the hotel and he put my bags outside the room in the corridor.

_Go downstairs and work in the lobby. You can pay for your own room. Plenty of potential customers down there for a New York model like you.

I was paralyzed with fear. I had nowhere to go. No one to call. He hit me hard with this sudden attitude and I saw he was mean, paranoid and jealous. And I had thrown in my lot with him. And burned all my bridges. My mind was racing and I saw two paths. One was to go downstairs not to work as a sex worker but rather as a thief. It was the packed lobby of the Hyatt Regency in Grand Central and commuters were buying drinks. I thought of the wallets filled with credit cards and cash.

I was an amateur thief and enjoyed the challenge when the stakes weren't so high. I stole for the fun and the high, and I never cared about the objects. The higher the degree of difficulty, the more I thought about how to take a thing. I liked money though not things. I liked the freedom money gave me. I knew people who were thieves for a living and I could bring cards and jewelry to them.

The other way was to get to the root of what was eating at him and talk my way back into the room. After a while I persuaded him and the reason for his outburst came to light. He had found a letter in my luggage. It was to a doctor in Texas who had helped me years before, asking him for a consultation. He was clearly crazy, but I didn't run. As I said, I had nowhere to go. The red flags were all there. I just ignored them. I just wanted my album to be released. I wanted a career in the music industry and I was ready to do what it took.

After all, I still believed he was somebody at Sony, and the only thing that was going to make this pain bearable, this life, was my record coming out and the validation a major label deal would be. I would play Madison Square Garden. I would talk to my security guards, show them pictures of my family....

- You see these photos, I'd say.
- These are my nearest and dearest, don't let them within 500 feet of me! Put them in the green room

> with a bunch of food and drink and let them watch the show from there. With my compliments! Oh, and make sure you pat down my brother. He goes armed everywhere.

I survived the years of the Disappeared in Argentina only to be disappeared by my family later on in New York so they could take my grandmother's money in court. I wouldn't have minded so much if they hadn't tried to take my life from me. They disapproved of everything I succeeded in and my Mother viewed fame like catching typhoid. They let me penniless in Europe when I was still practically a child, and when they all had millions. The state terrorists I knew in Buenos Aires lived in my house. If my stepfather didn't learn his methods of interrogation of a teenager from the Military Junta well, I just don't know. He was a natural born psychopath.

They spread rumors I had died of a drug overdose in the street no less, like Paul Newman's lover in Fort Apache The Bronx I dropped dead of smack walking down the street in the East Village mind you. They went into action with attorneys and trustees to confirm my death and I happily changed my name so I could be invisible to them. As soon as my mother brother and sister who hated my indifference to material things and to people's opinions, knew I had left with Manager Man from Sony they wasted no time to discredit me. I didn't frequent the same people and parties as I was busy working, always at clubs backstage or singing backup and I entered an entirely new world when I started recording my own music and I never looked back. The music business was captivating and all-consuming, so that I soon forgot everything before it. Before leaving, I handed my sister a stack of cash. All C Notes adding up to thousands of dollars. It was everything I had at the time. Then I didn't know on any level of my being how my brother and sister hated me for being strong, for going it alone. For being gone and out of the family's sick control.

When Agent Bellini came to the door my mother and stepfather went to town on me, knowing I had just won the lawsuit and settlement in Probate Court , they wanted me in jail or worse. They didn't say, she's with a really bad guy, can you help her? My father was by then in prison and I heard he told Agent Bellini

–My daughter is a thief.

Unlike my siblings who thought we were rich, in the way people were who let their money sit by and spent all the interest, are no longer rich. I never took money for anything and they were both high maintenance. My sister spent five full years at college with everything paid for by the family and never graduated. Once when I took her to lunch on Madison Avenue at my little spot, after a day of buying her armfuls of dresses in Bloomingdale's, she ended the meal by stealing my wallet. I only realized this years later, when she had stolen my inheritance money, my life, my online reputation, and even can't stay off my Pinterest and creeps on my pages grabbing images from me. It has been a jagged pill to swallow that my sister stood up in Probate Court and lied saying that she had actively looked for me, and she had not heard from me for seven years. It was easy for them to begin to establish the myth that I had died. I learned you can't disprove a lie.

I had grown up in my grandfather's threadbare apartment on Park Avenue. I was very happy as a child. I went to Hewitt, American Ballet School, and I rode at Claremont Riding Academy on Ninety-First Street. My grandfather took me to auditions on Broadway where he had been a producer when he was wealthier. My father was a real estate broker with a suspended Felony sentence for embezzlement. They had a spectacular divorce and my mother referred to him as His Majesty. He could not afford anything else as he supported his father. His father had been a clothing magnate and lost everything he had in the Depression and he had a lot to lose. He never saw it coming and all he had left of all his shops was five thousand dollars in the vault. He lost a grand lifestyle and all that was left of it was this tattered huge pre-war place out of Tolstoy's The Idiot.

When I was twenty-two trying to pay the thousands in bills my father told me he supported his father when he was twenty-four and I suppose that was true.

When I heard my father had died in prison I was paralyzed and in shock for years, so that this affected my personal relationships and decisions I've made in my life ever since.

*

We spilled out of the car in front of the Hasty Pudding Theatre. There was a party going on. The windows were thrown open and the Harvard students danced in the street to the music pouring out of the house. I looked behind me and there was no car following us, no one else driving on the street where light snow fell and I breathed the air and the smell of relative freedom. Light from the streetlamps sparkled and shimmered.

I was filled with joy. The joy of being alive and dancing in the snow on a winter night with the exuberant students, their lives ahead of them and all that fortune and the future held, and suddenly there was out of the sleepless nights, the choking fear and humiliation of being pursued by the FBI, the stabbing homesickness, the taste of betrayal and the worst bleakest storm I have had to withstand in my life, the distinct scent of possibility in the air The possibility I might get out of this alive. I joined in and danced away with everyone else in the middle of the street for fifteen minutes and then so as not to try Joe's patience, wandered back to the car.

- You're an immature idiot, he said.
- Yeah, well at least I'm one that isn't being followed. We did it!
- Good job. Now what?
- A place to stay. And no ID. That's a problem.

*

At some point when he went out I found in his files the evidence that nothing had changed. That it never would. He was running a house in the Back Bay and a female friend of his was acting as Madame. He was making thousands of dollars a day in cash but there was nothing in the joint bank account in which I had deposited my entire year's salary of thirty thousand dollars to finance the record.

It didn't seem like I was going to the Grammy's this year. I knew I was sitting on the X. I had better get a move on.

I visited a lawyer I'd made friends with in the music business and confessed the whole hot mess.

As I had predicted, he was not that impressed and didn't think it was a big deal to turn myself in to federal authorities. He was adamant I had to get away from Joe. He was confident I had a good career in store for me in the US music industry. The lawyer was personal attorney to a prominent performer and had just the one client. He has been to a few of my shows in Boston and told me it was just a matter of time before I was signed. He was right, no sooner did I start playing more shows and I had three record deals in my sights.

Suddenly I was standing, the argument was over, my attorney was back at my side and the Judge was talking. She mentioned my name!

- I spent the weekend reading the sentencing report and I can see that your client isn't taking responsibility for her actions. She blames everyone else.
- I am sorry for your family troubles, she directed her focus on me, but you went to Oxford, you knew what you were doing. Miss Carr I have decided to send you to prison for one year so you can think about your actions and…

Paul, my attorney was on his feet shouting…Your honor

my client is the victim here and she has suffered enough… once free of Joe Miller she has turned her life around. She regrets deeply what she has done. She can contribute to society in a very real way with her skills and languages…Don't punish her any more your honor!

I was breathing. I was meditating. I breathed in the stale air of the courtroom and the bad energy, sent it to my boundless heart where I burned it up into good energy and breathed it out in the form of gold bubbles into the fetid air. Tonglen. Sending and receiving meditation. I was going to prison. It was final.

What would my friend and boss at the hospital do for a year without me? I covered four languages on the floors and written translations. I worried about telling my boss who was so stressed out over this sentencing and waiting by the phone in her office to hear.

I imagined myself saying, Lola, I'm not coming back for a year. And before she could start protesting, I'd launch quickly into I've left you a spreadsheet of all the patients and their languages and weekly stats. It's on a flash drive in my desk drawer. And there's an English book there for Santiago, the boy who goes to the Burn Unit. And…

The Judge was talking.

- I am sentencing you to two years of Federal Probation. I am going to be in close touch with your probation officer Ms. Carr, and I can assure you that the slightest infringement of your conditions and you will go straight to jail.

Yes, your Honor. Thank you, your Honor.

- I sincerely hope the next time I see you will be at a cocktail party on the Upper West Side

And not under these circumstances.

- Thank you, your Honor.
- Oh Thank God, Lola my boss at the hospital said when I called her.

When are you coming back? I need you. It's chaos out there today.

*

The Honeymoon

As I walked out one evening, Walking down Bristol Street, The crowds upon the pavement Were fields of harvest wheat. And down by the brimming river I heard a lover sing Under an arch of the railway: Love has no ending.

WH AUDEN

- Distract the guards, he said.
- What's that? I asked.
- Distract the guards.

He scanned the horizon. We were at the port of Tangier in Morocco waiting to get onto the ferry to Spain.

The guards had gone inside with the passports and the ones outside were eyeing the brand new sparkling white Citroen Camel with Swiss plates parked there.

- Distract them from what?
- From the nine keys of hash in the car.

I tried not to react. I walked over to the guards and asked for a light in my bad Arabic. *Ahlan, Wasahlan…* It wasn't hard to be interesting in this situation, as I was dressed like a spoiled British school girl wearing a linen blazer white trousers and gold boots. We chatted and had fun laughing at my mistakes in Arabic. After what seemed forever in the hot sun the guards returned our passports to us and said.

- You may proceed to board Monsiour, Madame.
- Merci
- Bon voyage.
  We drove up the ramp onto the ferry to Algeciras and I could barely breathe.
  Drink in hand at the bar, I felt better.
- Seriously? I said, Nine kilos?
- Well it would have done no good to tell you in advance. Would it?

We had been married earlier in the month in Zurich.

We drove down in his new car to Morocco for the honeymoon.

His family owned the Hotel St. Gotthard in Zurich, The Palace in St. Moritz and The Continental in Lausanne with its nightclub so aptly named Hell. He could afford very nice cars and had plenty of money. He wasn't very generous with me though he made grand gestures like saving friends from going to prison by replacing the money they may have stolen. Or financing any kind of cocaine deal.

We stayed in Casablanca at a hotel with a pool and then at the lush Al Mamounia Hotel. He was a good driver and I enjoyed speeding along in the desert listening to music. On our last afternoon he said I should take a nap and he went out in the heat of the afternoon. I thought it odd at the time, and he said he wanted to check out the car before the long drive back.

He took me into Essaouira one day to the Café Central where we met the British author Paul Bowles for tea. He frequented the same place on the town square every afternoon in his white linen suit and straw hat. He entertained at his table anyone who spoke fluent English and I was a big genuine fan of his work. He talked about The Sheltering Sky and was pleased to find I had read all of his work including the short stories I admired a lot. It was a delightful time and we promised to write. I asked his advice for a young writer and I have never repeated what he said to anyone.

In Zurich he supplied all his friends and local musicians. My friends the American musicians soon became his clients, and they led to the bigger music festivals and more international clients. In the chain of supply for hashish, cocaine, and heroin, he was an experienced participant.

As for my part, he stepped up his game and I flew from Zurich to London to bring pills to a client, I went to Rome to bring back a load of pharma coke, I went back and forth to London and New York to bring hashish and brown sugar, cocaine. I looked the customs officers right in the eyes and lied, I did just fine.

He took me on buys when he found out I had a nose and could tell exactly what the product was. The drug business seemed to take all his time. The buys were dangerous in his view and he always gave me explicit directions as to what to do if he were arrested. He showed me how to try to save the situation if you had a lot of product on you, gain some time and throw it away somewhere you could come back for it.

There's no telling what attracted us to each other at Oxford. He was a student at a foreign language school. He was Swiss and he was taking part in a play directed by my cousin Amelia, in Oxford for a year from Princeton. The play was The Importance of Being Ernest. My cousin vouched for him. His best friend was seeing my good friend and roommate Vicky and soon we were all going out together in his Renault for meals in the country. There were wonderful restaurants around Oxford in the countryside as well as pubs.

That summer I had news from the United States that my mother, who had been battling cancer for some time, had died. Her husband, my stepfather had seen fit to exclude me from the funeral. My brother and sister had not protested. I had nowhere to put my grief. I fell in love instead with a man much older than me and a cynic. I was seventeen and getting no money from home. He promised to look after me. He soon encouraged me to withdraw from school and come to Zurich.

My husband and I were as different as chocolate and cheese. Sure it was exciting when he met me at Geneva airport and drove me to a famous bar called the Fox. He was already very high and driving like a fool. We drank Tequila shots all night and it was very romantic. The drive home not so much as I was sure we would crash. I am not a risk taker, which I know is funny considering the traveling and carrying and all.

From the time Andreas came into my life I had an entirely

new syllabus replace my traditional education. Drugs. He showed me how to prepare hash joints, cocaine joints, how to make lines, how to sniff cocaine and handle it. He taught me how to carry and how to exchange in public. He started giving me huge hunks of hashish that had to cost a hundred pounds and I would sell it off to my friends for pocket money. I no longer cared about my studies. I read novels all day long and avoided studying for exams.

One May morning after staying up all night we all piled into the car to join all the singers on Magdalen Bridge at dawn. Andreas took a wrong turn onto the High Street in the right lane and we were stopped immediately. Andreas was rude to the police who took him into custody and he missed breakfast at The Randolph Hotel. So there were signs of his narcissism early on which I ignored as we are prone to in our motivated reasoning.

Another time he dragged me out of a pub in the countryside, because he didn't like me talking to a flirtatious young gay friend. He was jealous. He drove back to Oxford in the Range Rover going way too fast and sometimes forgetting it was England, you had to drive on the left.

In Zurich he went out every night. I didn't find it interesting to go with him after a while as his companions were mainly coarse alcoholics, and I wanted sleep as I was looking for work.

Once he got so angry when I said I wasn't going out that he hit me and I fell on the floor. His friends in the other room came running in.

- Man, you should never hit a woman!
- You shouldn't hit her.

They helped me up and I didn't have to go out that night.

He had three DUIs and would have to spend three months in the Zurich jail. They would let him out during the day for work if he had a job. His father arranged something for him at the hotel owned by the family. I was so relieved to know he couldn't come home at night.

He still wanted me to work as a courier for him and I didn't trust him. I lost my nerve and threw out a package In the ladies room at Kennedy Airport because I didn't trust the situation. There was a police order to record our phone conversations so we used codes for doing business. The Zurich police were starting to build a drug case against Andreas. I wanted to distance myself from his business. Andreas was looking for a way out too. He started looking for a job in the US, taking advantage of my citizenship.

When we were in Oxford I noticed a pile of air mail letters permanently on his desk. I asked about them and he said they were from his ex girlfriend now in prison and assured me it was all over with them. On our first night in Zurich we ran into Anna and it was clear things weren't all over with them, not on her side anyway. She looked like she wanted to kill me. Strangely enough we later became distant friends and then friends. She sat on my bed and told me how she wound up in prison. Andreas had financed a big LSD deal and she had to go to England to bring it back.

She made it all the way to Zurich and out of the station

and into the square on the Niederdorf where the cafes are and she ran into an old boyfriend. She tells him what she'd been up to and he goes inside and calls the police. They arrest her with the entire load on her. They made a deal.She does the time and stands up for Andreas. He promises to marry her. His rich family had never accepted her humble beginnings according to her, and they would accept her. He never told her about me. She knew when she saw me that first night in Zurich that he had not kept his word. She said he wrote every week without fail.

Two days later I took the plane to Paris. I went to meet my father's new family at the Lancaster Hotel. I would tell them I wanted a divorce and I wanted to go home and return with them to the United States. I carried nothing but a packet of cigarettes in my pockets on the flight home and I did not have to lie to any official. My family refused to go through the same customs queue as me and I got through in five minutes while they had to wait an hour for my stepmother's Parisian purchases.

An American Model In Paris

When I was nineteen, I moved to Paris. I lived in a one room apartment, shared with a friend of mine from school, Nellie Cammott. The school I mean was the one in England from the past, because now there was a school of a different sort. We lived in the Rue Mouffetard on the third floor in a building with a Moroccan courtyard on the same street just doors down from where Hemingway had lived during his time in Paris. We had to climb a circular wood staircase up to the apartment. The floor and the ceiling in the place were slanted. The window was mediocre rectangle and gave out onto the street where the market would set up. We would see the mounds of fruit and rounds of cheese peaking out from under the awnings of the vendor's farm stands. We were always hungry, and we ate cheaply—pasta with butter and cheese, a cream sauce if there was a guest, wine, bread, coffee. Like that. We had plenty of money coming in really though the apartment cost us a very high rent of a thousand dollars a month and also we spent money on alcohol, wine, cigarettes, and drugs all of which were also very expensive—these things required a lot of income. They were habits we had got used to in the company of the wealthy boyfriends and men we had been with in England.

Those times were gone now in a sense, and we felt the loss. We knew though we never discussed it, that we were not part of the English aristocracy-a class you can only enter by birth or marriage.

The classmates we were friends with had many of them gone on to marry men with titles, castles, houses, yachts, horses and plenty of money to continue the life of parties, point-to-points and regattas without a thought as to how they could afford to go here and there and always a place to stay and money to either call home or go there often. I had none of these things and I never really thought about where I would be after university as I knew I wanted to teach and write. I had to find a way to do that. First I would need to learn how to live even if there was nothing I wanted to take away from the life lessons learned in Paris with Nellie.

Nellie was friendly with the man who collected the rent for the owner, the Principal at the American School who tried to give me a job even though I didn't know how to type. Poor man, he stood there transfixed by my feeble attempts at writing letters at the typewriter. I did not have the heart to assure hi I would learn. So I worked in a bar in the Rus St. Jacques on a tip from Nellie's friend On a cold sunny morning in Paris I presented myself to the owner at the Café St. Jacques which in the Rue St. Jacques around the corner from the Ecole Americain yet they have almost nothing to do with each other except for their proximity in the neighborhood. I did not see many of the well-heeled students from the American School going in there. The principal sent me messages through the students that came in. The bar was a place mainly for people who lived and worked in the quarter and at night it was a place for swarms of sailors and serious drunks. By nine the place was slammed and I left after midnight thanks to Nellie and her Roman boyfriend who came to haul me out of the grip of a bunch of drunk sailors.

The owner told me he was from Vietnam and had in Paris for twelve years. He offered to pay me wages of fifty francs a day and tips. I accepted. He was quite nice to me and his wife was angry when she met me and made me go clean the men's latrines. She set this as the first task I should have each morning at seven when I arrived at the café. I did not like having to talk to the men who sat for a long time at the bar during the day drinking their marc and coffee so I busied myself doing everything I could find. Once when I had my hands sunk into the hot soapy water to wash the glasses one of them said to me that I did not know how to work and that I needed to pace myself. Not to be working all the time. Always busy. That's no good. I believed him at first ad then I saw he just wanted me free to talk. The owner was receiving complaints that I was not friendly enough to the men, that I needed to smile more. He said I should stop looking busy unless his wife was present. He said I should think of wearing a low cut blouse or better yet wear the buttons on my shirt more open.

Nellie had a job in the Rue St. Denis. She was a house model for a fashion manufacturer. She went there every day more or less at nine in the morning. Her boss was not strict with her. She got up, made coffee, smoked a cigarette and got dressed in her mother's flowery St. Laurent peasant skirts and tall Russian boots. She was beautiful and she knew how to look at men so that they felt they were very important to her She did not have a very glamorous job as a house model as I learned one day when I went with her.

Right around then there was the story everywhere in Paris about the two American models who went out with some agency clients. They went to a chateau somewhere and these two ended up jumping out a window, and one broke her foot just to get away from these guys. Modeling is glamorous if you are protected and otherwise it can be very dangerous.

Everyone knows the modeling agencies in Paris are fronts for escort agencies. Even the most prestigious ones are there to lure young American models to Europe with the promise of a big ad campaign or contract. They give them one or two jobs and then they starve them. When they are desperate the agency offers them escort work. They are sent to entertain a French playboy. Some girls go home and many stay on, stuck in their daydream of finding fame and fortune in the editorial pages of Vogue.

*

Nellie wanted to introduce me to her boss to see whether he knew about any work for me elsewhere as he could not afford to take on another model. We were riding the metro to the Rue St. Denis from Censier Daubenton metro stop where we lived. I was in pain having recently pierced my nose with a diamond stud. It was getting infected I could feel it. The side of my nose was swollen and red. Nellie had made me dress up in a sweater and tight jeans tucked into high boots.

I had never asked her before and money was a real problem for me now. I had no bookings and wasn't likely to have them through my agency. There were tons of beautiful girls they could call.

She told me she made five hundred francs a day.

- Doing what? I asked.
- Oh you know doing things for him. Getting him coffee…she laughed.
- What? I asked.

Well, you know, I give him a hand a couple of times a day. I never do anything more.

- Well that's great.
- Oh come on. Don't be so pure.
- What do you mean? I just don't think you have to be a slave to a man for so little money.
- You mean you would do it for more?
- I don't know. I've never really thought about it. And I hadn't.

Nellie's boss was a fat ugly man and after a short coffee drinking session he took me in the back to talk business purportedly and grabbed me instead and tried to sit me on his fat thigh. I was curious as to what Nellie experienced every day and I could not see how she did it. Up close all I felt was revulsion and I got away from him. He was swearing at me when he came out of the back room. Nellie looked displeased when I came out and he followed sweating and swearing. The visit had not gone well. Nellie and I went to the nearby café for coffee and then she went back to work and I went home on the metro on my home.

*

On the way back to the apartment in the Rue Mouffetard from the café I found a pharmacy and bought some alcohol and cotton wool to deal with my nose piercing infection. I walked through the uneven streets in a man's overcoat my father might have given me. It was too large and I probably looked odd. People in the quarter would definitely look at me, and then again I had a diamond in my nose. I am not really tall or interesting to look at. I have my grandmother' pale skin and dark hair and my cousin says she is Sephardic and my uncle says emphatically that she is not. She died when we left for Argentina.

I walked carefully in my high heeled boots on the cobblestones. There was gray in the sky and the houses were so close together in the Latin Quarter. This was not the Paris I dreamed of without access to the clear sky and that incredible quality of light that is a blue sky in Paris. The sky in Paris is infused with so much light that you can see it is actually composed of tiny white particles and you understand why all the painters needed this light to paint by, writers need it to read and write by…at my place in the Latin Quarter there wasn't much light though. Even on sunny days the place was cold and dank.

This was not the Paris I had dreamed of from the city of my youth, Buenos Aires, which bears a strong resemblance in some of its neighborhoods to Parisian design and architecture. The Barrio Norte in Buenos Aires is filled with houses the French call hotels and petit-hotels, gray stone buildings some houses with balconies done in the ornate style of French houses. Not only were my surroundings ugly I was always tired and hungry .At home in Buenos Aires I had Studied and worked hard at school and I never had to worry where the next meal was coming from. I never got lost except when I wandered the city on my own which in Buenos Aires was rare and in Paris was the only way I got around. In Buenos Aires I had a driver and usually a bodyguard would come along. This was due to our being American on my mother's side and we lived in Argentina during a time when the dollar was very high bringing a huge exchange rate for the purchase of pesos when inflation was sky high. We were middle class in the United States and the exchange rate made my family very rich in Argentina, and they were not modest about their wealth. This was unwise at a time when Americans were hated politically in Argentina during the 1970s and when guerrilla warfare was taking place in the streets of Buenos Aires.

*

I was surprised when Nellie came home the next day with a name and a phone number of someone who knew someone at ChaneI had been looking for a sales job. Her friend had given it to her saying they were looking for a model like me. The number belonged to a photographer who was in Paris scouting for models for British Vogue. I made an appointment to see him a few says later. He was staying at The Hotel Lancaster in the Rue de Berri, near the Champs Elysées and the Arc de Triomphe. He was seeing models at the hotel.

The Lancaster is a beautiful intimate hotel built with a courtyard. It is furnished in period pieces and there are antique relic clocks belonging to the kings of France on every mantelpiece. The elevator is a gold cage and the carpets are lush and flowery. The staff speak impeccable English and are courteous beyond belief. No one blinked an eye when I walked in wearing a black motorcycle jacket black leather leggings and high heels. My hair was short and black and my skin was pale. I wore no makeup except when I was working. The hotel manager directed me to the third floor by way of the birdcage elevator.

The man who opened the door was gorgeous. He was blond with a round face and piercing blue eyes. He was blond, tanned, and his eyes were very blue. He stood looking at me with a wide grin on his face.

- Mariana? I'm Andrew. Come in.

He kissed me on the cheek the way Parisians do and turned and led me into his rooms.

He had a suite with a large sitting room. He had ordered tea and cake.

- I hope you eat cake?
- I adore cake!

We sat down and he poured the tea deftly like an Englishman and we had some, sitting at a small table in the living room, he on the chair and I on the sofa. He asked me about my life and my background and what sports I liked to play. He asked me if I would jump about the room and he showed me some pictures he had taken of a beautiful young blond woman jumping like crazy from the couch in the air. She wore a white tennis dress and tennis shoes.

- If you want to see me, who I am, I said, it will not be when I am jumping.
  He laughed.
- I think we're going to have to get high, he said.
- Why? I asked.
- Why? Don't you like to get high? He asked.
- What do you mean by high?
- You know, something to relax you and we can get into this thing. I think I would like to follow you about and watch your face when your expressions change. I'd like to photograph you like that, pensive, moody.

I laughed when he said this though later on I let him

take pictures wile we talked about literature and music, my favorite things. I started working for Andrew after that afternoon. I never went back to work in the Rue St. Jacques.

*

Sometimes when I came home in the evenings Nellie and her Italian boyfriend Vic were there. The place was only one room and I would sit at the table with them smoking a hash joint or I would try to sleep. If they were in bed I would sit at the table and try to read or write stories. The place was small and if a man called me up I would go out which was nearly every night. Sometimes Nellie and Vic would come along. The doormen in the clubs knew me by sight and they always rushed us in. We had some drinks, we smoked, we talked, and we had a good time.

*

One evening my father called me. We had just come in from a club at five in the morning.

`Next week is my fiftieth birthday, you know. I'm having a party in New York at The Regency Hotel. I want you to come. I'm sending you a ticket.

- Ok, I said.
- So, what are you doing with yourself?
- Working, I said.
- Doing what?
- Modeling, I said. I quit my job at the café.

- Well, if that's how you want to spend your time, I don't know…" he said.

I did not know what to say. What else was I meant to be doing?

- I'll see you next week, I said.

I hung up. The next day a messenger brought me the invitation to the birthday party and the ticket. It was round trip so at least I was not expected to stay in New York for long after the party.

*

When I got back to Paris I found out that the apartment was no longer mine. Nellie had given it up and gone down to Rome to live with Vittorio. My suitcase was in the basement of the American School minus some rather choice designer items I had got from working in the fashion trade. I found a room in a pension which I preferred to living in the agency's apartments with the other American models. Tant pis!

She Speaks to Angels

He will send his angels to guard you
They will lift you up with their hands
You shall not hit your foot upon a stone.

~Psalms

She speaks to angels~ says they all know her name.

The Black Crowes

One afternoon after a long nap, Adela woke to find the Angel Gabriel sitting in her room. It was a small room in a place on the Fifty-first floor of a modern Manhattan apartment building, which is called a condo, and seeing as this place was barely able to hold a bed, a table, a desk and a chair, the angel with his large shape and huge wings, seemed to occupy the whole space and breathe up almost all the available air.

She was very pleased to find that she had a visitor, as normally no one ever came to see her. She had been feeling rather lonely of late. Not that she was a recluse, no, she was an ambivert and a social person, and she liked to read voraciously, which led her to spend evenings alone. She was anxious, which she thought must be a sign of growing old, feeling fear, giving in to it now, as in the spring she had turned twenty-two. This fear which had come into her excluded her from her former attitudes and adventures out, so that she no longer would head down to the East Village at one in the morning for a drink in the A6 Bar on Avenue A nor would she go from there across the street to the Pyramid Club after tequila at the bar had warmed and enlivened her , where the transvestites danced up on the bar in shorts suitable for the Crazy Horse Bar , and the terrible bands tried to appear as nasty and tough as possible onstage and would scream in the back room and crawl and moan and writhe in the most believable attempts , and later when they got off stage and drank and spoke with the people hanging there they were all rather scared and sweet. She wouldn't walk to The World's End on Second Street and Avenue B, to hear the really loud House music and see the stars shimmering here and there in the crowd. There Madonna and Jean Michel Basquiat could be seen, on any night of the week, and Sinead O'Connor, Robert Palmer and all six Spanish Vogue Models from his video Addicted to Love. Upstairs and downstairs, pushing and shoving as if the other destination were important almost essential to one's existence; they went there every night so did it matter where they stood to view the stage or each other ~yes! No doubt it did. Here Sinead O'Connor played an impromptu show one night at one in the morning. Upstairs the club owners in their Brooks Brothers coats could be seen stuffing trash bags full of cash into the ceiling at every interval.

The old cavern of a theatre was crumbling about their ears, yet no one seemed to notice or to care. The well-dressed crowd from Soho and extremely well-dressed crowd from uptown , meaning much further north than fourteenth street , and possibly ,only fifty-second would draw the line here , would mingle with artists from the East and West Villages and Tribeca , and Soho bankers , and gallerists, and British and American music managers in mean leather jackets shiny and trashed , and black boys from Brooklyn in bicycle gear sharing crack in the VIP room upstairs with beautiful young white girls. The women stood in close groups, close to the men, enjoying protection, and they wore short shiny dresses the color of grapes or silver, and very high heels. The men kept their hands on the women touching them in a proprietary fashion. There were the women artists in leather jackets and trousers , skulking about anonymously , sometimes with a husband in tow ,and there were the dowdy wives of the famous male artists , eyes drinking in the sight of the fashion models tall and graceful slim:·calla lilies in a pond of mud , amidst the common crowd , so extraordinary they were , and everyone admired them , and other beautiful young ones could be seen in smoky dusky air of the interior of that club well after two or three in the morning on any given day in the city.

There could be seen several nights a week a young girl with pale skin and eyes lined heavily with black her hair piled on top of her head the color of ink, a tattoo on the back of her neck that reads **reve** and men surround her hanging on every word, even though here, no one can hear anything that is said. There is a young man in a daze at the end of the bar, feeling lonely, smiling when he sees someone he knows even when it is not a friend who approaches him. His partner is at home tonight dying any day now of AIDS. When he walks home from Tribeca later he chants as he passes the West Village buildings, dying, dying, dead. Dying, gone, dying, as he passes the homes of his friends.

*

The entire place had a smell of crack, mixed with the odor of sweat. The result was a complex perfume, and there was a true mixing of different classes, from those who worked to amuse, by sweating onstage, and those who came solely to admire. Next to the aura of this cloying, rather dirty life of the night that Adela usually led if you counted all the drinks and cigarettes in the little black and diamond holder , this life of the night that Adela usually led and glorified to the point of calling it the Bohemian , the sight of the angel was a shock in that he seemed both so clean and so serene. And he was very handsome. He had a classically beautiful face.

*

The angel just sat there, while she wondered if she might get past him to make tea.

- Would you like some tea? She said.
- Yes, that's fine, he answered in his nice voice.
- I hear you've been very confused lately -said the Angel Gabriel, his voice clear and booming, sweet, not scary.

He spoke with a bit of a British accent.

- You've been a bit down lately, haven't you?

- I despair of humanity she said.

She must be in a dream. The angel's eyes were cold and blue. They sliced through her like knives. He was older than she had imagined. much older, and very gracious as well as graceful.

For a big angel, he was certainly very light on his feet. He told Adela he had loved to dance in his youth.

The Angel turned and looked out the window. Here on the fifty-first floor New York was spread out below like a floating blanket of cloud and haze and the sky was pale whit. There was a deep silence in the room. Not even the rush of traffic was heard.

She began to cry. A quiet, constant streaming at the eye, that was even worse for being silent.

She held and kissed the Angel's hands.

- Thank you for bringing my faith to life, and for comforting me in my terror. I just want to know what to do, how to serve. Where to put my energy? Do something worthwhile on this planet.

He returned her embrace. He held her slim face in his hands.

He was the absent father she never met, he was her protector, the one she had never had.

- I love you, Adela, he said.
- I love you too, she replied.

*

She waited for him outside the The Barbizon Hotel where she had tea with her Mother. Then they got into a taxi as soon as he stopped in front of her to greet her and take her by the arm.

- The Plaza - he told the man.
- We'll go to the Oak Bar-he told her. He wore an Italian suit of English cloth .and smoked Silk Cuts. As they walked the loudly carpeted corridors towards the bar he took something out of his breast pocket and gave it to her. It was a piece of paper with an Ode by Petrarch he had copied out for her birthday.
- This is for you - he said.
- Thank you so much - she said

They sat down at a table near the window and he called the waiter over by directing him a look of extreme self-assurance.

- What will you have, the man said.
- What do you want? Jay asked.

I don't know -Adela said. She crossed her hands in front of her.

- I'll have a martini, why don 't you try one?
- Alright -she said.

He gave the waiter a nod. The man hurried away.

She took a cigarette in her hand. He lit it for her. He

lit one for himself. He crossed one leg over the other and looked around. The room was not crowded. It was after ten.

*

The next day she woke up in the bedroom that had been covered in plastic. The sun filtered through and the dust could be seen in the shadowy light. She was alone and next to the bed stood the book of Emerson he had been reading to her the night before while they smoked a cigarette of Benson and Hedges tobacco and strong black hashish.

She did not know where he had gone. She looked about the room which was entirely made of plastic and inhaled the scent of the good fabric of his wool jackets and shirts that were made in Italy which he just brought back. She felt embarrassed when he came in just them, she had been lost in thought when he appeared, and she turned away from him to get dressed quickly.

- I've brought you coffee -he said.
- Thank you.

She was dressed very well in her black suit. He looked coldly at her. She put her hands in her hair self-consciously. He sighed as they walked towards the door. He walked her to the door and kissed her, a dry kiss on the cheek.

*

The autumn morning was cold and she walked for blocks in Tribeca, and along Canal Street toward Chinatown. She stepped along in the stiletto heels of the night before in a black sheath dress and a thin black coat. She turned left off Canal Street and went north into Soho, on Greene Street. The day was raw and the wind felt wet as it touched your face. Halfway up the block she stopped for a man in a suit wearing long dreadlocks. He was dressed very well in Armani and wore a lot of jewelry on his fingers and wrists.

- Addie- he said.
- Troy-she said.
- You can always tell the true beauty of a woman by the shoes she wears- he said.
- Oh, can you? she said.
  They walked along, side by side.
- You will come to my place for coffee? he said.
  She went along. It was about 11 am.

He lived on Fifth Avenue, above the One Fifth where she sat and drank with a man she knew from Zurich who lived in New York now and sometimes they went there together for a Bloody Mary on the way to the studio. They were both musicians. She was spoiled though, she lived with a man uptown who took care of her. A drunk, with a lot of business problems who was mean to her, and so she suffered, only not from actual hunger.

- The trouble is, the Swiss one told her, you've never had to worry where your next meal is coming from.
- No I've not, she said.
- People think it's easy once you solve the problem of survival, she would say, but for some, the struggle starts there…

- Oh nonsense, Rudi said. You don't know what it is to go hungry·

Troy's place was small, just two rooms and a tiny kitchen, and it smelled of burnt cocaine and cigarette. He took her to the bedroom where there was on one chair, and she sat on the bed. He sat in the chair at the desk, rolling joints of good marihuana and arranging rows of cocaine, which he took to her where she sat on the bed, holding the mirror for her while she bent over, using her long shiny nails to put it in her nose. She smoked many cigarettes. They drank cold water.

- We should go out to tea-she told him.
- Yes, maybe that would be best, wouldn't it? he said, looking at her.
- Why, what is it? she said.
- Well, I know you are involved in another sadism, he said.
- You could call it that, she said.
- And what would you call it? he said.
- What is this? said Adela. Let's go.
- 0h but wait, he said, I wanted to ask you, you have a lot of rich friends, and also when you model, he said, or act, or sing, so look, you give them this, Ok?
- You want business from them? I don't know. I think not.
- Look, I want to show you my closet, he said. Inside were at least three hundred

Armani suits and as many pairs of Italian shoes.

- It's beautiful, Adela said.
- We could go out, and I could dress for you.

- Just go out? she said, No sadism?
- Yes, yes, he smiled. His face was imposing and around it fell the long tiny twists of hair, his eyes were bright, and he had the smell of jasmine.
- Fine, she said.

*

As it was Saturday night it took a long time for the cab to get downtown to Sounds of Brazil on Varick Street. It was raining; the streets were slick and wet. She found him immediately as the big man at the door took her by the arm and escorted her to the back where Troy had a table and was waiting.

He was not alone; the table was filled with other young elegantly dressed couples, from the Caribbean and from the Bronx. The music was loud and there was a salsa band playing and people were dancing and shoving to walk or stand and there wasn't a centimeter you could move without being on top of someone's feet. The air was ripe with smoke and the waiters drew rounds of applause when with agility and guts and brains superior to their audience they wound through the insatiable crowd to deliver a trays of drinks at a table.

She drew the attention of the other women, who all stopped talking in turn, to get a look at her. She liked their appearance, even though they intended to be jealous of her, she knew it would be a fun evening, and she sat down smiling. Taking her hand to his mouth, Troy kissed the fingers.

- You see how it is here -he said.
- They know you-she said.

They sat and drank. He filled her glass. She counted three times champagne and after that lost track. Troy got up one time when he was gone for half an hour. When he came back he offered her a cigarette. She smoked it until her head hurt. She passed her hand across the forehead and leaned toward the table on her other arm.

- It has base-said the man next to her.
- What? Adela said.
- Crack. It's a paste. He puts it in those cigarettes.

This was an Italian man who spoke to her. She'd met him once in Troy's company and they had spoken once or twice in passing on the street outside Troy's building. He said he did hair but Adela knew he was a drug dealer just like Troy and she liked his tall big body and his red hair.

- Unbelievable-she said.
- Yeah, he's bad-Giulio said.
- I think I don't feel well she said, I think I'll go.
- I'll take you, he said.
- Would you, that would be great, I live uptown.
- Ok… Do you want to go this way.

He held her as they pushed through the crowd.

She woke up the next morning in the pink bedroom on Fifth Avenue with the redheaded man beside her.

- Oh God! she said, panicking. What did we do?
- Nothing, we did nothing, he said.

- Why not? she asked him.

You weren't feeling well, you passed out, he said.

- Thank God! The whole night is a blur. Thank you for bringing me here. How did you do it?
- In my BMW. You were still awake. You passed out here.
- Oh. What a drag.
- Not at all.
- Shall we get some breakfast?
- Yes let's.
- I take it your uncle's not here.
- No he isn't! she laughed a hearty laugh. Her head felt better. She wanted to see Jay. She wondered if he had wanted to call her. He wouldn't do it though when she lived with her benefactor, and he knew that wasn't her uncle.
- Adela, Adela, he said, why do you search for troubles?
- I don't know. I have nothing to lose, she said.

The Italian man, Giulio, drove them to Brooklyn to a big diner in Bay Ridge. She liked the glass display of pastries and cakes and the hot coffee the servers with such high hair like in a movie, and the families out together. She was very small next to Giulio who was so big and she laughed a lot and listened to his stories about growing up with his grandmother in Brooklyn and going to Manhattan at fifteen to be a fashion stylist for the high fashion industry and doing a *stage* at Ungaro in Paris.

*

She called him up.

- We're in the kitchen; we're making couscous for thirty people. Do you want to come on Thanksgiving?
- I'd love to.

But she didn't go.

She stayed with Ray. They went to the Regency Bar and he got drunk and fell asleep on the couch. He barely spoke to her at lunch, and grumbled at the three hundred dollars for lunch with so many bottles of champagne. He depressed her so much, she went back to her room afterward and just sat there, staring out the windows at the view of Central Park, she watched the sun go down and it was beautiful. Her eyes filled with tears and after she cried she felt much better.

*

She went to dinner with Jay at Kotos several days later.

- God I'm so glad to see you, she said.
- Are you?
- Yes, he's a madman, she said.
- Well, maybe you should start seeing other men, he said.
- Maybe I should, she said.
- The other night there was a party-he told her while they ate the sushi, and there was this really beautiful oriental girl. She works for Oscar de La Renta, and we were talking and she came downstairs with me,

and it was really nice, except she had capped teeth, but other than that she was very pretty.

- Yeah except then she got really jealous when she came on Thanksgiving and I spent the whole time talking to Susan, but she and I have something, I represent her now, and we're friends, and you know it's strange because twenty isn't all that different from forty…and we're talking about art and Mary is getting annoyed. So I offended her.
- Yes I can see.

They drank sake with a Saporo beer chaser.

- You didn't come, he said. Why not? -I was ill, she said, with the flu.
- Oh, he said, and now you're fine, yes?
- Oh yes.
- Good. Because I'm in good shape too,
- Good, she said.

They ordered red bean ice cream.

They walked to his loft in the cold together. She held his arm. The wind blew their hair in their faces.

- Now I suppose you want flesh.
- I want to smoke, she said to him when he spoke to her.
- Well, that's all the way on Christopher Street.
- Never mind then.

*

The Angel Gabriel sat and contemplated her small face.

- You are better off on your own, and you will get where you are going much better.
- He travels fastest who travels alone, Adela said.
- The desire of the moth for the flame of the night for the morrow, said Adela.

She told the angel everything that afternoon with the sun slanting through the blinds and beyond the view of Central Park and its canopy of trees. She told him all the things she thought she knew about herself.

Hours passed.

- How I enjoy discussing this with you.
- And with you, I know.
- Well there are some things though I can't stop thinking about when I try to get to sleep, which is why I don't sometimes if I haven't been writing and I'm not exhausted, is why did the Holocaust have to happen. I mean after that you can't possibly believe, can you. And look what part modernity had in it.Because it wouldn't have been possible without the modernization of warfare. and the industrialization of the world. And God is certainly not able to explain ….or rather He is not going to…

She looked to see his beautiful face in the light that filtered through the blinds.

- I think you should sit in the sun more-the Angel

said to her. You are too identified with Pluto, a tiny planet at the furthest edge of the solar system, now why would you want to be identified with that?

- I wouldn't, she said. She wasn't sure, really.
- Exactly, and you'd want to be out of the darkness, and into the light, to the center. That's what I know you should do. Sit in the sun more, close your eyes and imagine the sun. See yourself in the light.

These words made her laugh musically for a moment, she looked away at the bed.

- I am so tired, she said.
- Of course you are. I'm sitting right here while you fall asleep.

And when she woke up, he was gone.

*